Hoofbeats drew his attention back to the present, and he turned around.

Lottie rode in on Bella, pulling the mare to a stop just outside the barn. The woman sat a horse well and rode like she'd been doing it all her life. A wide smile brightened her face, and the sun gleamed off the yellow braid hanging down her back. Why couldn't she be as ugly as three-day-old stew and as mean as a cougar?

It would sure make things easier for him. Sighing, he walked toward her and held Bella's bridle as Lottie dismounted.

"Fine day for riding." Lottie smiled and patted her horse on the neck.

"Yep, it is." Brett led Bella into the barn, hoping Lottie wouldn't follow. He put the horse in her stall and swapped the bridle for a halter, then gave her a bucket of feed. Lottie followed and uncinched the saddle. She started to tug it off, but Brett reached for it.

"I'll get it." His hand landed on top of Lottie's, and his gaze met hers. He should move away, but his feet were stuck, as if trapped in quicksand.

"Uh. . .thanks." Cheeks flaming, Lottie tugged her hand free and picked up a brush.

Brett ducked his head, certain that his ears matched her red cheeks. What was he thinking, staring at Lottie like that? The problem was, he enjoyed working side by side with her. What would it be like to do that every day? To wake up beside her? To hold her close each morning?

Brett wished for a bucket of cold water to douse his head in. He yanked off the saddle. The only way he and Lottie would ever be together was if he joined her in a jail cell.

VICKIE MCDONOUGH believes God is the ultimate designer of romance. She is a wife of thirty-three years, mother to four sons, and a doting grandma. When not writing, she enjoys reading, watching movies, and traveling. Visit Vickie's Web site at www.vickiemcdonough.com.

Books by Vickie McDonough

HEARTSONG PRESENTS
HP671—Sooner or Later
HP716—Spinning Out of Control
HP731—The Bounty Hunter and the Bride
HP747—A Wealth Beyond Riches
HP816—Wild at Heart

Don't miss out on any of our super romances. Write to us at the following address for information on our newest releases and club information.

Heartsong Presents Readers' Service
PO Box 721
Uhrichsville, OH 44683

Or visit www.heartsongpresents.com

Outlaw Heart

Vickie McDonough

Heartsong Presents

This book is dedicated to the people of Medora. To those who founded the tiny town and stayed when life was so difficult there. And to those contemporary visionaries who sought to preserve Medora's unique history and refused to allow it to die out like so many other small towns have throughout history. Please forgive any fictional liberties I took in places where research was unavailable.

Also, to my critique partners, who faithfully proofed this and made it better with their creative suggestions: Susan Page Davis, Margaret Daley, Therese Stenzel, Jan Warren, Gloria Harchar, and Caron Smith.

A note from the Author:
I love to hear from my readers! You may correspond with me by writing:

Vickie McDonough
Author Relations
PO Box 721
Uhrichsville, OH 44683

ISBN 978-1-60260-265-6

OUTLAW HEART

All scripture quotations are taken from the King James Version of the Bible.

All of the characters and events in this book are fictitious. Any resemblance to actual persons, living or dead, or to actual events is purely coincidental.

Our mission is to publish and distribute inspirational products offering exceptional value and biblical encouragement to the masses.

PRINTED IN THE U.S.A.

one

Rocking M Ranch, Southwestern North Dakota, 1894

"You want to do what?" Quinn McFarland shoved his hands on his hips.

Anna resisted the urge to squirm under her brother's stern glare. "I want to find some type of employment."

Shaking his head, Quinn spun around and looked out the parlor window with his arms crossed over his broad chest. No doubt he was thinking of all the work he had to do and that he didn't have time to humor his little sister. He turned, slow, like a cougar about to pounce on its prey. "That's utter nonsense. We have more than enough money and plenty of work around here. Women are supposed to work at home, not someplace else."

She knew he wouldn't understand. Anna plopped onto the parlor's settee, thinking that was the longest string of words her somber brother had said in a week.

She loved their large log cabin and helping Quinn around the ranch, but something was missing in her life. How could she make her work-all-the-time-never-have-fun brother understand how she felt? Why, Quinn practically woke up the roosters each morning.

He rubbed the back of his neck and sighed. His dark brown eyes, so much like hers, softened. "Look, I realize you feel a bit lost since Ma's been staying at Grandma's for so long. And now Adam is gone, too. I can't pretend to understand the connection you two have, being twins and all, but finding employment isn't the answer."

Anna stared at her hands. What he said was true. While she loved Adam's new bride, Mariah, she missed her twin terribly. He talked with her and joked. He knew when she felt sad, and if she was bored, he'd find something to challenge her mind or body. All Quinn did was work.

Twisting her hands in her lap, she glanced up at him. "It's been hard to lose Adam—"

"We haven't lost him. He'll be back."

"It's not the same. He has a wife now. He doesn't need...me." Thick with emotion, her throat tightened. She poured herself a cup of tea from the pot that sat on the low table in front of the settee. The cup clattered on the saucer as she lifted it.

Adam had found the love of his life and was finally realizing his dream of drawing the West. His wife, Mariah, wrote dime novels for a Chicago publishing company, so traveling with Adam gave her the opportunity to get fodder for her stories. Anna was truly happy for Adam, but his leaving had left a hole inside her that nothing else could fill. Even praying hadn't helped.

"Have you written Ma about this crazy idea of yours?"

Anna couldn't look him in the eye, knowing she hadn't mentioned her desire for a job to her mother. Mama would have had the same reaction as Quinn. Hadn't she left her own children—albeit grown ones—to care for her ailing mother? She'd never understand Anna's longing for something different to do.

"I can tell by your lack of response that you haven't." He paced to the dining table and back into the parlor, his long legs making quick work of the short distance.

"I have an idea." Quinn snapped his fingers, crossed the room, and stood before her. Dressed in denim pants, a blue chambray shirt, leather vest, and boots covered in a layer of dust, he looked every bit the rancher that he was. His dark blond hair even had a perpetual ring-shaped indentation from where his hat had pressed it down. "I hadn't mentioned this to you yet, but I'd planned to take our annual trip to Bismarck next month to stock up on supplies before winter comes. What if we go earlier? Maybe this coming Monday? We can visit Ma and Grandmother for a few weeks."

Anna set her teacup on the table and jumped up, clapping her palms together. "Truly? Oh, that would be wonderful! They'll be so surprised to see us this early."

She dashed around the table and embraced her older brother. He was solid, hard muscled, and a good three inches taller than Adam. Not one to overly show emotion, he lightly embraced her and patted her back. She looked up at him and smiled. "Thank you, Quinn."

He cleared his throat and stepped back. "I've got work to do."

"Me, too. I've got to get busy so I'll be ready. Three days is hardly enough time to prepare." All the things she needed to do before leaving raced through Anna's mind. Pack. Make a list of food supplies. Search the catalogs for anything else they would need over the long, cold North Dakota winter.

"We can wait and go in a few weeks, like I'd planned, if it's too much of a rush."

"No! I'll be ready."

Quinn chuckled and shook his head. "Make your lists. Don't forget ammunition and restocking the medicines for the animals. I'll have Claude write down what we're needing." He grabbed his hat from the peg near the front door and left.

Anna hurried to her room and threw open the wardrobe door. Fluffing the skirt of one of her wool dresses, she noted its thinness. She'd need to buy a new winter dress or two and another split riding skirt, and she and Leyna, their cook, needed to make a long list of food supplies.

Excitement surging through her, she grabbed the stack of catalogs from the floor of the wardrobe and hurried to the dining room table. She loved going to Bismarck to visit her grandmother and to shop, and she couldn't wait to hug her mother again. Oh, how she'd missed her. A smile tugged at Anna's lips. And just maybe, if she worked things right, she could find employment there and not have to come back to the boring Rocking M Ranch.

᛭

Standing outside of the U.S. Marshal's office in Bismarck, Brett Wickham rubbed his thumb over his deputy marshal's badge. Was he really ready to resign? To call it quits and go back to ranching with his younger brother?

"You sure about this?" Taylor watched him. "I'd love to have you back at the Bar W, but if you're not ready to quit, we can get along without you for a while longer."

No, it was time. Brett had put months of thought and prayer into his decision. He was ready to live a slower life. After five years of chasing outlaws, his ache for adventure had been satisfied. Two dollars per captured outlaw would never make a man rich, but then he hadn't done the job for the money. He'd served the state of North Dakota by capturing numerous thieves and murderers and seeing them convicted for their crimes and making life safer for the decent folk.

"I'm sure. It's time I went home. You still got the draft from the cattle sale?"

Taylor patted his shirt pocket. "Right here."

Brett nodded. "You did a good job getting that herd here. Why don't you go to the bank and get the cash for the draft while I tender my resignation. Then we can celebrate with a steak dinner."

Taylor smiled and rubbed his belly. "That's my kind of celebration. After I go to the bank, I'll find my wranglers and pay them their wages, and then I'll meet you at that little café across from the hotel, all right?"

Brett nodded and watched Taylor amble away until a wagon

loaded with supplies blocked his view. His younger brother had been a skinny, pimple-faced kid when Brett left their Bar W ranch to realize his dream of becoming a lawman, but now Taylor was a man. His brother had stepped up when their father died and kept the ranch going. It was time now for Brett to go home and shoulder some of the responsibility.

Maybe if he was lucky, some pretty gals had moved into the area or some of those giggly schoolgirls he used to tease had grown up. He smiled, remembering how he'd tied a frog to one of Sally Novak's braids. The girl had squawked and thrashed like a chicken chased by a fox. Yep, he was ready to settle down and have some ornery boys of his own, but a man needed the right woman to do that.

The window on the door rattled as he stepped inside the marshal's office. The scents of leather and gun oil mixed with cigar smoke. Brett nodded at the young deputy seated at the desk. "Marshal Cronan in?"

"Back there." The man jerked his head toward the rear office.

Brett saw his boss, Marshal Joseph Cronan, seated at the desk, his head down, as he studied a wanted poster. Brett knocked on the doorjamb, and the man looked up. His mustache twitched just before he smiled. He stood, offering Brett his hand. "Caught any more criminals, Wickham?"

They shook hands. Brett sat after the marshal did and hung his hat on his knee. "Not since yesterday."

Marshal Cronan chuckled. "Well. . .I don't reckon we can catch one every day, though I'd sure like to."

Brett let his gaze rove over the various posters mounted on the wall to his right. The office was rustic, messy, and reeked of cigar smoke, but that didn't keep the marshal from doing his job.

"So, ya ready for a new assignment?"

Brett resisted the urge to fidget like a schoolboy in trouble. He hated disappointing the man who'd been his mentor. "No, actually I've uh. . .decided to. . .uh. . .resign."

Whew. That was harder to get out than he'd thought.

Marshal Cronan pursed his lips and studied him. He narrowed his eyes for a moment; then resignation dulled his gaze, and he sighed. "Real sorry to hear that. I sure hate to lose a good man like you."

"I've got a younger brother who's been running the Bar W since our pa died. It's time I go back and do my fair share."

He nodded. "A man's gotta do what he feels is best. I wish I could offer you a fair wage to stay, but. . ." He shrugged one shoulder.

Brett knew the deal. A marshal risked his life for his job. He didn't make a wage and only got paid if he captured and turned in an outlaw. If he and the outlaw were killed together, the marshal's family was expected to pay the burial expenses of both men. It wasn't right, but that was the way of things.

Brett laid his badge on the marshal's desk. "Thank you for taking in a rebellious youth and making a man of him."

The marshal nodded. His chair squeaked as he stood and shook Brett's hand again. "I've got train robbers, cattle rustlers, and the Sallinger gang acting up again. I'm hoping you'll change your mind."

Brett flashed him a wish-I-could-help-you smile, slapped his hat on his head, and walked outside, feeling freer than he had in a long while. Yes sirree, time for a new beginning.

❧

Anna walked along the street that angled down a steep hill, taking in all the sights and sounds of Bismarck. The town seemed to sprout buildings as fast as her garden did weeds. Every time she came to visit there were new houses and stores going up.

Anna enjoyed having her mother walk beside her after being separated from her for over a year. Ellen McFarland still turned heads at forty-seven. They greatly resembled one another with their blond hair and brown eyes. Anna hoped she looked as youthful when she was her mother's age.

"It's too bad Quinn had to return to the ranch so soon. I'd hoped he could rest and visit more than a few days." She looped her arm through Anna's. "I missed you so much."

Anna smiled. "I missed you, too. Are you staying here much longer? Grandmother seems to be doing better."

Her mother's cheeks turned red, and she looked away. "You children are grown now. Adam's married." She stopped and faced Anna. "I'm not sure that I will be returning to the Rocking M."

Anna's heart fluttered. She wasn't coming home?

"I can see this comes as quite a shock to you, darling. Mother is doing better, but I don't feel she should be living alone at her age. I'd love for you to stay here with us for the winter."

Anna started walking again. Was this the answer to her prayers? Her loneliness? Could she leave Quinn alone to run the ranch?"

Her mother took her arm again. "It's a lot to think about. You don't have to decide right now. Let's just enjoy our time together. There's a wonderful little shop a few blocks over that has all manner of feminine accessories. They have the prettiest hair combs."

Anna thought of the long list of supplies she would have to purchase now that Quinn had returned home, and she found it difficult to get excited over a hair comb. People dressed in fancy clothing passed them by on both sides of the street. The large buildings blocked the view of the hills unless she looked up the street. She missed the wide-open spaces and quiet of the country.

"I do hope Quinn will be all right. I pray for you children every night."

"It's been a long while since we've had rustlers. I hope we didn't lose too many head of cattle. At least they didn't get any of the Percherons." Anna swatted at a fly buzzing her face.

"I worry about Quinn out chasing rustlers."

"He'll be careful." Anna flashed her mother an ornery look. "What he needs is a wife to settle him down."

Her mother smiled, brown eyes twinkling. "It will take a very special woman to do that."

"And a mighty patient one, too." They shared a laugh.

"If we don't find a dress you like in one of the stores here in Bismarck, we can try looking in Mandan."

"I'm not that picky. I'm sure I can find something here." Anna jerked to a halt as a man rushed out the doors of the Bedford Hotel and nearly plowed into them. He marched down the street without so much as an "excuse me."

Her mother shook her head. "Whatever happened to manners? I declare, some of the folks these days don't know how to show even the simplest courtesy."

Anna scowled at the rude man and pulled her beaded reticule, the small handbag she saved for trips to Bismarck, farther up her arm. "Most of the cowboys on the ranch are quite polite, but we do occasionally get one who isn't. Quinn soon puts them in their place if they act improper around me."

"He's a good brother. He did a wonderful job of keeping that ranch going after your father died. I still regret not helping him more, but I was suffering my own grief at the time. Besides, Quinn was always determined to do things himself."

They ducked into Harper's Mercantile. Anna's eyes took a moment to adjust after being in the bright sunlight. The scents of leather, coffee, and spices filled the air, exciting her. Purchasing such a long list of supplies was a big job, but her interest peaked seeing the new items that the stores in Bismarck carried.

Her mother had offered to make her a skirt, and Ellen fingered a charcoal gray wool, but Anna's eyes drifted to a dark green.

"Has it been hard for you since Adam and Mariah left?"

Anna shrugged, not wanting to burden her mother with her worries. "I do miss him—both of them, if you want the truth. Mariah quickly became the best friend I'd never had."

"She's a lovely woman and seems to be the inspiration that Adam needs. I'm glad I was able to go to their wedding." Ellen smiled as if remembering the ceremony held in the tiny church in Medora last summer. "At least you know they'll be back for part of the year. That should be a comfort."

"Yes, it is." But it would be a long time before they returned from their travels. Too long. "I've been thinking of trying to find some kind of employment."

Her mother swiveled around, staring with her mouth gaping open like a widemouthed bass. "Don't you have enough to do at the ranch? It's most unusual for a woman to work unless she's a widow with children to support or a schoolteacher. Really, Anna, that seems an absurd idea."

Anna sighed. Her mother's response was the same as Quinn's. Why did it matter if a woman worked outside the home? Surely there were jobs a woman could do better than a man.

"Would you live in Medora?" Ellen shook her head. "Besides, you wouldn't want to leave Quinn all alone, would you?"

Hadn't Ellen just asked her to do that very thing by inviting her to spend the winter in Bismarck? And how could she explain that Quinn was the one who deserted her? He worked away from the house all day, and in the evenings after dinner, his head was either in a book on cattle breeding or ranching techniques, or he was checking her bookkeeping. He simply didn't know how to relax.

"Why don't you stay a few months here with your grandmother and me? We could have such fun. There are so many more things to do here than on the ranch."

Maybe an extended change of scenery would do her good. But did she really want to be in a crowded town for so long? "I'll think about that."

"Do you see anything you like here?"

"What about the emerald?" Anna was glad to be on a different topic.

Her mother unrolled the bolt of green wool and held it up in front of Anna. "It looks good with your coloring, although a brown or gray would go better with your eyes."

"I think I will get this. I love the color."

They purchased six yards of the wool cloth and several other items then meandered out of the store. The streets of Bismarck were crowded with people. The one thing Anna disliked about the city was all the noise. People chattered everywhere, harnesses jingled as wagons passed on the streets, and the smells were so different than those of the ranch.

"I need to stop at the bank and make a withdrawal. Then what do you say to eating lunch at a café?" Her mother tugged her across the street toward the Bismarck Federal Bank.

"Oh, I'd love to." Anna nearly bounced. The only time she ate out of the house was at a church social or when she came to town. It was a treat that she eagerly looked forward to.

They crossed the street and headed for the bank. Anna helped her mother up the steps and reached for the bank's door handle. Suddenly, the doors burst open. Someone rushed out and plowed smack into Anna. She gasped and spun around, snagging her heel on her skirt, and fell down. The other person tripped and landed beside her. Gold coins exploded from a bag and plunged to the ground like shiny raindrops, clinking onto the boardwalk all around her.

Heart pounding, Anna looked up and caught the angered glare of the other person who'd fallen—a woman's glare. The woman jumped up and grabbed the bank bag, which looked to be only half full now, and raced toward a nearby horse.

A shot rang out from inside the bank, and the door flew open again and clanked against the wall. A poorly dressed man with a full beard charged outside, lugging two more bank bags and waving a gun. He glanced down at Anna and the coins lying all around. The gun turned her way, and her heart dropped. Her mouth went dry. *Lord, help me.*

two

The outlaw's gun hovered in Anna's face for only seconds, but it seemed a lifetime. Her breath caught in her throat as her heart stampeded. The man muttered a curse and ran to his horse, pocketing his weapon. Anna's whole body trembled, but she heaved a sigh of relief as the two outlaws galloped down the hill.

A skinny man with round spectacles ran out the open door. "Bank robbery. Stop them!" He shoved his hands to his waist as he watched the two riders disappear around the corner at the end of the street.

People from all around hurried toward the bank. The clerk looked down at Anna and scowled. His eyes widened when he saw the coins on the ground. "That money belongs to the bank."

He grabbed her arm and attempted to pull her up. "Someone hold her until the marshal comes."

Anna jerked her arm away. "No, wait. I didn't have anything to do with the robbery." As if she were telling a falsehood, a coin rolled off her lap and clinked against one already on the boardwalk.

When no one moved to hold her, the clerk pursed his lips and dropped to his knees, frantically gathering up the coins.

Anna rubbed her aching wrist and remembered her mother. She twisted around, relieved to see her standing by the bank window, holding her handbag to her chest, shocked but safe.

"May I assist you, ma'am?" An older gentleman offered Anna his hand.

"Yes, thank you." She reached out to him, and as she stood

on trembling legs, gold coins dropped from the folds of her skirt, plunking onto the boardwalk. "Oh, dear."

The clerk scowled at her again. "That's the bank's money."

"I—" Anna started.

"Listen here, Floyd," the man beside her said. "This woman is an innocent bystander. I saw it all. That first robber plowed out the doors and knocked this woman in a tizzy. The bank bag fell open, spilling coins everywhere. You should thank her. In a way, she actually saved some of the money by causing that first thief to drop the bag."

The flustered clerk's cheeks reddened. He picked up the last two coins and cradled them all in his untucked shirt. "Sorry, ma'am."

A heavyset man shoved his way out of the bank and looked from side to side. "A man's been shot in here. Somebody get a doctor."

❧

Brett glanced at his pocket watch and resumed staring out the window. He'd been waiting nearly a half hour for Taylor to arrive for lunch. He must have had trouble finding his crew.

Brett sipped his coffee, marveling that he could be so relaxed after finally quitting law enforcement. Out of habit, he glanced at the others in the room, studying their faces, still remembering all the wanted posters he'd viewed on nearly a weekly basis.

"Can I warm your coffee?" A young woman offered him a coy smile.

He held up his cup, enjoying her pretty features and fresh look. "Thanks."

"Do you want to go ahead and order or keep waiting for the rest of your party?"

Brett shook his head. "I'll wait. He should be here at any moment."

The café door rattled as a big man fumbled with the knob.

Finally, he shoved the door open and searched the room. His gaze landed on the wiry man at the table next to Brett's.

"Doc! You're needed at the bank. A customer was shot during a robbery," the burly man shouted, not even taking the time to cross the room.

The man at the table beside Brett's jumped to his feet, tossed some coins down, and left his half-eaten meal. He hurried from the café, his napkin still tucked in his waistband.

Brett went rigid. The bank. A customer was shot in the bank?

He leaped up, dropping a handful of coins on the table, and raced for the door. His mind pounded out a cadence with his fast-moving feet. *Not Taylor. Please, God, not my brother.*

A group of people crowded the bank entrance. The doctor tried to shove his way through. "U.S. marshal," Brett shouted. "Clear the way."

The crowd parted like the Red Sea had for Moses, and Brett followed the doctor inside. He blinked his eyes as he searched the room. Near the counter, a man lay on the floor. Brett's chest tightened as he stepped forward.

The doctor knelt beside the man and checked his pulse. He shook his head and stood. "There's nothing I can do. He's already gone."

As the doc stepped to the side, a force equal to a cannonball hit Brett in the gut.

Taylor.

His brother lay dead on the floor. The bank draft for their cattle was still clenched in one fist, and his gun lay on the floor a few inches from his other hand. Brett dropped to his knees.

No.

Not now.

Oh, God, why? He fought back tears. A marshal never cried. He scooped up Taylor's still-warm form and hugged it to his chest, fighting back a moan. As he held his brother's body in his arms, he listened to an account of what had happened. Taylor had simply been in the wrong place at the wrong time.

"If'n that young cock hadn't gone for his gun, he'd most likely be alive right now," a skinny clerk with round glasses stated.

Brett clenched his fist. He wanted to clobber the man for referring to his brother in such a way. Taylor was mature for his age and honorable as the day was long. If he'd gone for his gun, it was to protect the others in the bank.

Brett pulled the draft from Taylor's fingers and pocketed it, berating himself for not cashing it himself. But Taylor had been the one who had raised the herd and driven it all the way to Bismarck. It was his place to reap the benefit.

Some benefit.

He lifted his brother and stood, Taylor's limp, muscled body weighing heavy in his arms. Brett clenched his jaw so tight it ached. Numbness kept his feet from moving, and his vision blurred as Taylor's blood soaked Brett's shirt.

Marshal Cronan left a group he was questioning and strode toward Brett. "You know him?"

Brett blinked, struggling to make his clogged throat respond. "He's my brother."

The marshal's eyes widened. "I'm sorry, Brett. Can I do anything for you?"

"You can give me my badge back."

"You sure?" The marshal pursed his lips, his mustache twitching.

Brett nodded. "Just let me get Taylor to the m—mortuary." He nearly choked on that last word.

"You need help?"

Brett shook his head.

The marshal nodded, understanding that this was a job Brett needed to do alone. "I've gotta find Charley Addams.

He draws sketches for me. From the descriptions, it sounds like Jack and Lottie Sallinger robbed the bank. I want to get clean drawings of them before the witnesses forget what they look like. I got a poster on Jack, but nobody's ever gotten a good look at Lottie until today."

The crowd of murmuring spectators stepped back as they walked outside. Brett hated their sympathetic stares and curious glances. How could things change so fast? Could he ever go back to the ranch knowing his brother wouldn't be there?

The first thing he had to do was bury Taylor. He nearly stumbled at that thought. His younger brother had always followed him around, wanting to be like Brett. And yet, Taylor had stayed home while Brett ran away from their overly strict pa and put his life on the line as a lawman. He should be dead, not Taylor.

Brett bit the inside of his cheek until he tasted blood. If it took the rest of his life, he'd hunt down the Sallingers and vindicate his brother.

❧

The next day, Anna pored over the ads in the newspaper, finally settling back in her chair, discouraged. She had hoped that if she stayed in Bismarck for an extended time as her mother had requested, she might find some kind of employment here, but it was no use. She heaved a heavy sigh. Nearly all the advertisements were jobs for men, and the ones that weren't sounded boring or involved too much work for the puny wages offered. Though Anna loved children, she had no desire to be stuck in a building teaching them all day. So what was a woman to do? She could be a cook, seamstress—if she learned to sew—or clean houses, pretty much the same things she had done back home.

Flipping the paper closed, her gaze landed on an article about the bank robbery. She scanned it and gasped. The description of the female thief sounded just like her. Had that buffoon of a clerk given the law officials a description of her instead of the outlaw? She'd seen the woman up close, and she looked nothing like Anna except for their hair coloring. She'd never forget those cold hazel eyes glaring at her.

Anna shivered. She'd acted brave yesterday in front of her mother, but the truth was, that robbery had frightened her more than she could ever remember being frightened—and she wasn't one to scare easily. She'd read in the paper that a young man had been killed, a rancher from southwestern North Dakota. A man not even as old as her twenty-two years. How sad to die so young. So needlessly.

She felt the city closing in on her, strangling her. Anna longed for the open fields and high buttes of her Badlands. A place where one could ride for days and never encounter another person. Where the only sounds were those of nature. And yet, she didn't want to leave her mother. Who knew when she'd see her again?

"I so hate to see you go. You barely just arrived." Her grandmother lifted Anna's beaded handbag off the coffee table. "What do you have in here? Stones? It feels like you brought half the Badlands with you."

Anna giggled. "A gal needs her stuff, doesn't she?"

"That she does." A smile tugged at her grandmother's wrinkled cheeks, then faded. "I do wish you'd reconsider staying longer. I so enjoy your visits."

Anna patted her hand. "Why don't you and Mama come to the ranch and stay awhile? It would do you good to get out of town for a bit."

She shook her head. "No, these bones are far too old to withstand the shaking and rattling of a train all the way to Medora and then taking a long wagon ride to the Rocking M. I'll just have to content myself with waiting until you visit again in the spring. I do thank you for sharing your mother with me. I don't know how I would have gotten along when

I broke my leg last year if she hadn't come to help me. I like to pretend, but in truth, I know I'm not as strong as I was before that happened."

Half an hour later, after hugging her grandma good-bye, Anna left with her mother for the mercantile. She still had numerous items to purchase and arrange to have shipped back to Medora. Once she was done, she would hightail it home, away from the hustle and bustle and accusations of this town. Maybe by next spring, things would have quieted down and she could plan a long stay in Bismarck.

⁂

Brett stacked his small pile of supplies on the mercantile counter and looked around the store. He still needed to fill his tin of matches, pick out a new shirt to replace the one that got ruined when he carried Taylor's body to the undertaker, and get more cartridges for his Winchester.

Along the wall, he grabbed an extra large, blue chambray shirt and headed back to the counter, his boots echoing on the wooden floor. Two young women batted their lashes at him, and he tipped his hat to them.

"I need a box of those cartridges," he told the clerk as he pointed to the brand he wanted.

The bell over the entrance tinkled and a shadow darkened the doorway as two women entered side by side. Brett nodded to the older woman and turned his gaze on the younger female. His heart nearly jolted out of his chest. Lottie Sallinger?

He ducked his head and turned. Surely she wouldn't be so brazen as to march into a store the day after robbing the Bismarck Federal Bank. Out of the corner of his eye, he watched her examine a shelf of spices. The older woman stayed by her side like a shadow, chatting merrily. Were they related? Or merely friends?

He ambled to the window, feigning interest in a fancy tooled saddle on display. From his shirt pocket, he pulled out the sketch of Lottie Sallinger. The woman in the store looked exactly like the drawing. His heart pounded, but his thoughts warred with each other. Hadn't Marshal Cronan said this morning that the Sallingers had been spotted south of Bismarck?

And Lottie Sallinger wasn't a lady, from all reports. So could she be playing the part of one as a daring, elaborate disguise?

He studied the woman then looked at the picture. The same oval face with a small straight nose and pleasant lips stared back. Of course, he couldn't see the color of the woman's eyes, but he wondered if they weren't the same brown as Lottie's were reported to be.

The two women took their armloads of purchases to the counter. The clerk scooted Brett's measly pile over, and his eyes gleamed as the women deposited theirs.

"I have a list of supplies that I need filled and delivered to the train depot by ten tomorrow morning. Will you be able to fill such a large order?"

The woman's voice was soft, delicate. Not at all what he would expect in an outlaw. That Lottie Sallinger was quite the actress.

Imagine the guts it took to order a wagonload of supplies in the same town you'd just robbed. Would she pay in double-eagle coins, like those missing from the bank?

"I can handle this just fine. What name do you want on the crates, ma'am?" The clerk held his pencil poised for her response.

"Rocking M Ranch. Medora."

Medora? Was that where the gang hid out when not on a robbery streak?

He'd been through the sleepy little town in the heart of the Badlands. Wasn't much there. Some big, old factory that a French nobleman had abandoned after his business failed and a handful of smaller buildings east of the Little Missouri River.

Now that he thought about it, the Badlands was the perfect place for a hideout, except maybe during their frigid winters.

Should he arrest her now or follow her, hoping she might lead him to her brother—and the stolen money? And who was the older woman?

He couldn't even collect the money owed him for the cattle sale since the bank had no funds at the moment. But that was the least of his worries right now.

Brett rubbed his thumb and forefinger down a fancy leather belt. His last arrest had gone bad when he'd gotten in a hurry and hadn't taken enough care to gather the proper evidence. The outlaw had been set free, and he quickly kidnapped the thirteen-year-old daughter of the man who'd testified against him. Brett clenched his jaw, remembering the day he'd found her battered body. He released the crimped belt.

Lottie was at the counter, counting out a stack of dollar bills.

Brett didn't want to make the same mistake again. He'd never forget having to tell that girl's parents that she was dead. The mother's cries still haunted his dreams. This time, he'd use caution and patience and make sure he had the evidence needed to convict the Sallingers—and see them imprisoned and awaiting trial for killing his brother.

three

With an ear-shattering squeal and hiss, the train shuddered to a stop. From his inconspicuous seat at the back of the train, Brett watched Lottie collect her few belongings and stand, as did the other half dozen passengers who were getting off at this stop. Clothed in a dark blue travel dress with her golden hair caught up in one of those net things, Lottie looked more like a woman going to church than an outlaw. But looks could be deceiving. Brett stood and stretched, gathered his saddlebags and rifle, and plodded down the aisle after the last passenger had disembarked.

He spotted Lottie a few cars down, talking to the baggage clerk. She waved her hand at the boxcar in front of her, then turned and marched down the street.

Brett watched her, then glanced back at the cattle car. He needed to follow Lottie, but he also had to claim his horse before the train left. It would take the baggage handlers awhile to unload all the Rocking M crates he'd seen at the Bismarck depot, but he couldn't take a chance on losing Jasper. Brett jogged toward the baggage handler and gave the man his claim ticket. "I've got a quick errand to run. Just tie that big black gelding up over there"—he motioned toward the hitching rail in front of the depot—"and I'll get him when I return."

The man nodded. Brett handed him a couple of coins and hurried past the depot. He looked both directions and finally saw Lottie at the far end of town, going into a big barn he assumed was the livery. He walked past two buildings and leaned against the sidewall of a barbershop. He hoped Lottie was fetching a wagon for all those supplies she'd bought in Bismarck so she'd have to return to the depot, but if not, he wanted to make sure to see in which direction she rode as she left town.

He glanced around as he waited. Medora hadn't changed much since the last time he'd ridden through. The town was tucked in a nice little valley with tall, rocky buttes surrounding it. The Metropolitan Hotel was still the largest building in town, unless you counted the abandoned meatpacking plant just east of the Little Missouri River. A handful of houses surrounded a pretty whitewashed church with a steeple and stained glass windows.

After several minutes, Lottie came out of the livery driving a two-horse team hitched to a buckboard. Brett admired the matched pair of stock horses pulling the wagon. Sure enough, Lottie headed straight for the depot. Brett moseyed down the street, keeping his eye on her.

While she parked the buckboard, he got Jasper. The gelding nickered to him and stuck out his big head for a scratch. Brett obliged the animal, slung his saddlebags over Jasper's rump, and shoved his rifle into the scabbard then tightened the cinch.

Lottie climbed down from the wagon, said something to the baggage handler, and then meandered down the street. The man beckoned another worker, and they carried a crate from the baggage car to the buckboard. Brett stopped at the depot's watering trough to allow Jasper a drink and watched Lottie enter a café.

His stomach gurgled, reminding him it had been a long while since breakfast. Next door to the café, he tied Jasper to a hitching post and then entered the small restaurant. Lottie sat at a table along the wall. A heavyset woman dressed in a faded brown calico covered with a stained apron stood beside her, rattling off the food items of the day. Brett ducked his head and sat at a table two away from Lottie's against the rear wall.

With her back to him, he hoped she wouldn't notice him.

"Afternoon. Coffee?" A short man held out a coffeepot and pointed at the mug on Brett's table.

Brett nodded and turned over the cup. "What's good here?"

"Stew, chops, beans, and corn bread." The man shrugged one shoulder. "Most everything."

"I'll take a bowl of stew, and could you wrap up some extra corn bread so I can take it with me?" Who knew when he'd get another chance to eat?

"I can do that." The man disappeared behind a stained calico curtain, and Brett could hear the clatter of pans and murmur of voices.

A woman dressed in a white shirtwaist and brown skirt came through the front door. She glanced around the room, and her gaze zeroed in on Lottie. She smiled and walked up to the outlaw's table. Brett couldn't see Lottie's expression but was sure she stiffened. He leaned forward in his seat, hoping to learn something that would help him locate Jack Sallinger.

She cleared her throat. "Excuse me, Miss McFarland."

Lottie looked up. "Good day, Thelma May."

They exchanged pleasantries for a few moments.

"Care to sit down?" Lottie asked.

Thelma May shook her head. "I don't want to bother you, and I need to get back to the dress shop. I just wanted you to know we're having a sewing bee at the Parkers' home on Saturday while the men are raising a new barn. I wanted to invite you and your brother."

The plump woman Lottie had been talking to earlier breezed past Brett, carrying a plate piled high with roast beef, potatoes, and corn bread. The fragrant scent wafting in the air nearly did him in. The woman nodded to Thelma May and set the plate in front of Lottie.

Brett wished he'd gotten the roast beef now instead of stew. The old man who'd taken his order plunked a bowl in front of him, gaining all of Brett's attention. His mouth watered as he took a bite.

"Well. . .I know you're not overly fond of stitching, but I wanted you to know that you're invited." Thelma May hoisted her handbag up her arm.

"Thank you. I'll let Quinn know about it if he's back. We've had trouble with rustlers."

Quinn? Was that Jack's alias? Brett mentally filed away the name as he shoved half the square of corn bread into his mouth. His lips quirked up at the ironic idea of outlaws having problems with rustlers. In a matter of minutes, he wolfed down the whole bowl of stew. It wasn't the best he'd had, but it was filling. The plump woman topped off his coffee, and he stared at the black liquid.

He still couldn't grasp in his mind that Taylor was dead. Just when Brett was ready to settle down. He remembered his father's stern discipline and how all he'd wanted when he was in his teens was to get away. After a brief stint as a sheriff's deputy in a small town, he knew he wanted the freedom a marshal had, rather than being tied to one place all the time. It had taken a long time for him to grow up and face his responsibilities, but after giving his heart to God, he was finally ready.

So why would the Good Lord allow his brother to be gunned down, especially now?

Brett couldn't wrap his mind around the thought. He was a fairly new Christian, and except for when that freed outlaw had killed that young woman, Brett's life had been good. He'd been happy for the first time in a long while. Lonely, but mostly content.

Brett sipped his coffee. He should have seen to Taylor's burial, but he sent his brother's body home with the Bar W hands. They'd make sure he was buried next to their parents. Guilt gnawed at Brett for not taking Taylor home himself, but he couldn't let the Sallingers' trail grow cold.

He glanced at Lottie's table, and his heart skittered. She was gone!

His gaze darted to the window as he lurched to his feet. Relief washed over him when he saw her outside talking to a bent old man.

"That Anna McFarland sure is a looker," the man who'd waited on him said. " 'Course, that older brother of hers won't let no man near her. It's unusual to see her in town without an escort."

So he was right. The Sallingers lived somewhere near Medora. Brett sidled a glance at the man. "What can you tell me about the Rocking M Ranch?"

"Depends. Why you want to know?" He narrowed his faded blue eyes and wiped his hands on his dingy apron.

Brett shrugged. "Heard it was a good place to work. Just wondered if that was true."

The man visually relaxed and nodded. Brett kept his gaze traveling between Lottie and the man.

"The Rocking M is a good-sized spread—around three or four thousand acres, from what I've heard. Them McFarland brothers raise several cattle breeds and Percherons. Got some of the best draft horses in this part of the country. 'Course, Adam got married last year and ain't at the ranch now."

Adam? There were two Sallinger brothers? He'd never heard that before. "Have they owned the ranch long?"

The old man shook his head, sending the few hairs on his bald head to dancing. "Their pa bought out a bunch of small ranches back in '88, after two of the worst winters we've ever had in these parts. Lots of ranchers lost most of their herds. Plumb closed down that meatpacking plant just across from Little Misery."

Brett knew the snide nickname referred to the tiny town just across the Little Missouri River, but this was the first he'd heard of the Sallingers' pa being alive. "So I need to talk to the older McFarland about work?"

"That'd be right hard to do since he's dead. Quinn's the man you want. He's tough but fair."

"How did Mr. McFarland have enough money to buy so much land?"

The old geezer shrugged. "Scuttlebutt says an Irish uncle left him a fortune."

Brett saw Lottie wave at the man she'd been talking to, and then she headed out of view. He laid some coins on the table. "Thanks for the meal."

"Oh, hey, forgot yer corn bread." The man darted behind the stained curtain.

Brett tapped on the table. Lottie couldn't move fast with a heavy wagon, but he didn't want to lose track of her. The trail from her wagon wheels could get lost among all the wheel marks in the rocky dirt from other wagons driving through the town. The man hurried toward him and handed Brett a package wrapped in waxed brown paper—still warm.

If he'd had time, he'd have picked up a few more supplies at the local mercantile, but trailing Lottie was his priority. Hopefully by tonight, he'd have the Sallingers in custody.

Then maybe that aching hole in his heart from his brother's death would begin to heal.

⋙

"Whoa!" Anna pulled the wagon to a stop in front of her home. The log structure was big compared to many homes in the North Dakota Badlands, but it was rugged, like the weather here. It may not have the attractiveness that the fancier homes in Bismarck had, but it was far better than a soddy or dugout. And best of all, nobody here would confuse her with a bank robber.

"Afternoon, Miss Anna." Claude scratched his shaggy beard. "Boss man didn't say nothing about you returning home so soon."

Anna set the brake on the wagon and climbed down. "He thought I was staying longer, but I had an aching to come home."

He grinned, revealing his crooked teeth. Claude wasn't a handsome man, but his heart was full of God's love. He even spoke at the Sunday services they had at the ranch sometimes when there wasn't a minister in town. "I'll get Hank and Toby on this wagon. Where you want them to put all these crates?"

"The porch off the kitchen is fine for now. Leyna and I can unpack them and put things away. Most are food items. Those three"—she waved at the trio of crates on the bottom of the pile—"are for the bunkhouse. Cookie will be happy with all the spices and other things I purchased."

Claude rubbed his belly. "I reckon we'll all be happy if'n we get to eat somethin' other than beans and corn bread."

Anna laughed and headed for the house. Inside, she hung her hat on a peg near the door. After being in the bright sunshine, she could barely make out the shapes of the parlor's furniture, but the scent of the house was familiar. The delicious fragrance of baking bread made her stomach grumble, even though she'd eaten just a few hours earlier.

"Leyna, I'm home."

The middle-aged German cook hurried through the kitchen door, smiling. An apron covered her dress, and her typical braids were curled up in two big buns, pinned on either side of her head. "*Fräulein* Anna! I not expect you home so soon."

Anna hugged the woman who'd been more like a dear aunt to her than an employee. "I'm glad to be home again." She pushed back, grinning. "And just wait until you hear what happened to me."

Leyna looped her arm through Anna's. "Come. You tell Leyna. *Ja?*"

"The men are bringing the wagon around to the mudroom. Oh, just wait until you see all the wonderful things I bought.

We'll be baking all winter."

"We?"

Anna grinned and shrugged one shoulder. Leyna's thick accent made "we" sound like "ve." "All right, *you'll* enjoy using all the spices and canned items I bought."

"I should teach you cooking."

"I'd rather be out herding cattle or working with the Percherons." She poured herself a cup of water and drank it deeply.

"One day, a young man will take you to be wife. You will wish you know cooking and sewing then." Leyna waved a wooden spoon at her.

"Quinn won't let any man get close to me long enough for me to get to know him well enough to marry."

"The right man will not let that *störrisch* brother of yours stop him."

"My point exactly. Quinn is stubborn and hardheaded." Although she couldn't help wondering what kind of man could best her strong, capable older brother. That she'd like to see.

"We have rustler trouble. *Herr* Quinn has been gone since he returned from Bismarck, chasing after those bad men."

"Did the rustlers get many cattle?"

Leyna shrugged. "What do I know? Those men, they do not talk with me." Murmuring something in German, the cook snatched a towel off the back of a chair and pulled two golden loaves of bread from the oven. Anna's mouth watered, but she worried for her brother and hoped they hadn't lost too many head of cattle.

After a snack of warm, buttered bread, they set to the big task of opening all the crates and putting things away. Two hours later, Leyna stretched, pressing her fists to her back.

"We will eat good this winter, but I must fix supper soon or we not eat tonight. Ja?"

Anna wiped a damp towel over her hot face. "I'm not too

hungry after unpacking all those crates. Why don't we just eat sandwiches tonight?"

"*Nein.* Sandwiches not enough. I make soup." Leyna turned away and washed her hands in a basin.

Anna knew it was useless to argue. Leyna might claim Quinn was stubborn, but once the cook set her mind to something, there was no changing it. "I'm going riding."

four

Following Lottie Sallinger had been more difficult than Brett had expected. Not because she didn't leave a clear trail, what with that wagon loaded down with supplies that she'd paid for with the robbery money, but because of the landscape. The rocky plateaus atop the buttes gave a clear view ahead, but if Lottie so much as turned her head, she'd have a perfect view of him.

There was little brush tall enough for a man on horseback to hide in and precious few trees. He felt grateful that the location of his ranch wasn't this barren. At least there were plenty of grasslands among the rocky terrain here for cattle to survive on. The Badlands held a rugged beauty of its own. Wind-whipped rocks in colorful layers similar to tree rings looked as if a giant knife had sawed off the side and left the guts exposed. Oranges, greens, browns, and even some black layers created a majestic display of God's handiwork. Above, a *V* of Canada geese headed south, honking at the world below.

Brett dismounted and climbed to the top of the next hill. Lottie's trail had disappeared in a pass between two tall buttes. Brett crept through the grama grass and stuck his head up behind a small sumac bush.

He sucked in a breath at the unexpected sight. A green valley boasting a nicely laid-out ranch with a huge log cabin spread out before him. Smoke curled from the chimney, lending a deceptively peaceful, homey touch. There was a decent-sized barn, also made of logs, and a few smaller outbuildings. Whoever built this ranch must have hauled those logs a long ways and was determined to meet the harsh elements of North

Dakota's weather head-on. Brett couldn't help admiring the spread but found it difficult to believe outlaws could have put in the work necessary to build such a place. His own ranch was a far cry from this. Of course, his place was built with sweat and hard labor, not with money stolen from innocent people.

Brett thought of Taylor's cold, limp body and clenched his teeth. The Sallingers had to pay. He wouldn't allow them to live as though nothing had happened. His world would never be the same. The temptation for vengeance was strong, but he knew that was wrong, both in the eyes of the law and God's eyes.

Justice. That's what he must focus on.

"I know, God, 'Vengeance is mine, saith the Lord.' But would you really mind all that much if Jack Sallinger got killed?"

Brett winced. Some Christian he was.

For a half hour, he watched two men unload crates from the buckboard and set them onto the porch. Then they drove the rig alongside the barn, unhitched the team, and carried the last of the crates into what he assumed was the bunkhouse. All he saw of Lottie was when she'd step out onto the side porch and set another empty crate on the pile.

Brett wrestled as his ire grew. Good, decent folks had put their hard-earned money in that bank, and the Sallingers just helped themselves to it. Even when he caught them, most of the money would be gone. 'Course, there was this fine ranch that could be sold to make up the difference.

Lying low on the ground, Brett kept watch. A few men came and went from the barn but none went into the big house. Was Jack out working for the day or off somewhere robbing someone else? And why had he left Lottie unprotected in Bismarck?

Maybe he should just ride in and capture Lottie and use her to bait Jack. Maybe he could get the drop on the few wranglers he'd seen and pick them off one at a time, especially since they weren't armed.

He rubbed his eyes and yawned. Grief and anger had over-powered his sleep the past few nights. A thick fog muddled his brain. "Help me here, Lord. Let me avenge Taylor and capture the Sallingers so they don't harm anyone else."

A sharp rock poked his belly. He fished it out and tossed it aside. A lizard zigzagged away from the spot where the rock landed. Brett rested his chin on his arm. No one could see him if he kept low, but he worried about someone stumbling across his horse. The ravine he'd tethered Jasper in hadn't offered much in the way of concealment.

Though the day was cool, the sun bore down on his back, warming him. Brett scratched his whiskery jaw and yawned again.

A horse's whinny jerked Brett awake. His blurry eyes focused, and he saw Lottie riding away from the house. He slithered back from the edge of the butte and hurried to Jasper. Was she going to meet Jack? Could he end this chase by tonight?

⁂

Anna loped her mare across the flat grasslands. The wind-sculpted buttes of the Badlands encircled her. Most folks would see nothing but a wilderness unfit for human habitation, but the odd combination of thriving grasslands and rocky barrenness reminded her of the Bible, where it talks of God creating life in the desert.

If one was tough enough, he could forge a good life here, but it was never easy. Snow could either fall twelve months out of the year or the temperature could be so hot you could fry an egg on a rock. Anna loved the challenge of surviving against the odds, but something was missing in her life. Something she hadn't noticed until her twin left.

She reined Bella to a walk near a four-foot-wide creek, a tributary of the Little Missouri that ran just west of Medora.

After a hot, mostly dry summer, the creek ran low, sputtering its way over the myriad rocks and pebbles that made up its bed. Such a peaceful, soothing sound after the noise and feverish pace of Bismarck.

Anna dismounted and tied Bella to one of the cottonwoods hugging the creek line. She started to reach for her rifle but felt sure she'd be safe without it this close to the ranch. So many people coming and going kept most critters away, especially in the daytime.

Sitting on a flat, sun-warmed rock, she sighed and thought about her disastrous trip to Bismarck. "I was a ninny, Bella. Hightailed it out of town as soon as I could after that bank robbery. Ma probably thinks she did something to upset me."

She'd never come so close to death as she had when she'd stared into that robber's pistol. The moment had only lasted a few seconds, but it had rattled her to the core. Then to have that buffoon of a clerk accuse her of being a partner in the robbery—just because that lady thief knocked her down and dropped coins all over her.

Anna shuddered, pushing the horrible memory away. She had more important things to think of, namely finding something to fill her time. Oh, sure, Quinn let her help out with the cattle and horses, but more and more he seemed to be pushing her to do womanly things instead. But what did she know of cooking and sewing? All she'd ever wanted to be was like her brothers. Now she wished she hadn't fought Leyna so much when the woman had tried to teach her to sew. It might be nice to make a colorful quilt during the long, cold winter to occupy her time.

The cool breeze blew a strand of hair across her cheek, tickling it. She brushed it behind her ear. Scratching her neck, she looked over her shoulder, feeling uneasy, as if someone or something was watching her.

Oh, stop it!

She'd been on edge ever since that robbery. A black-and-white magpie squawked at her, drawing her attention back to the creek, before it went back to hunting for its dinner.

Anna laughed and picked up a pebble and tossed it in the water, splashing a few sprinkles on the bird. The magpie scolded her and flew over to another rock a dozen feet away. Anna smiled at the creature, wishing she had a bread crust to give it.

Maybe she needed to focus on getting a husband instead of finding employment, which she doubted her stubborn brother would allow either. But the spouse pickings were few in Medora. Most men of the marrying type were already settled with a wife, and the men who were left hardly inspired a young woman to matrimonial aspirations.

Anna heaved a sigh. She loved the Rocking M, but life was too lonely here. Picking just the right man was essential, and she wouldn't trade one bossy man for another. Maybe she could get lucky and marry someone like Adam, who was traveling the West, drawing his wonderful sketches. Maybe a merchant, but definitely not a rancher, or a banker, whose life could be snuffed out by robbers.

What she really needed to do was pray instead of trying to work things out for herself. Claude had preached recently on letting God ordain man's steps. She'd wanted to get employment in Bismarck, and look how drastic things had turned out there. Anna looked heavenward. "Show me what to do, Lord. Give me a direction for my life."

She closed her eyes and prayed, realizing now how she'd given in to her fear and fled Bismarck. The question was. . . should she go back and try harder to find employment? Or had God sent her home for another reason? She began humming and soon started singing "Amazing Grace." That song never failed to touch her heart.

A noise across the creek snagged her attention, sending the

magpie to flight. Anna sat up, suddenly quiet. Listening. Her heart pattered. A half-grown bear cub poked its head past a clump of junipers and sniffed the air. It waddled toward the water and stared right at her. Bella snorted and pawed the ground.

Anna stood. Cute as it was, she would have enjoyed watching the creature, but where there was a cub, there was a mother bear. Bella whinnied and pulled at her reins. Anna jumped off her rock and jogged toward her mare.

The bear cub bawled and backed up at her sudden movement. A loud roar answered back, and the angry mother plowed out of the brush and lumbered across the shallow creek straight for Anna.

☙

Brett followed Lottie to a creek bed where she tied up her horse and then sat on a flat rock. Was she waiting for someone?

He crept down the boulder he'd been hiding behind, edging closer, careful not to make a sound. If she did meet with someone, he wanted to hear that conversation. Lottie sounded as if she were humming. It baffled his mind how a lowdown outlaw could be happy enough to hum.

Not to mention be so pretty. Her golden hair was now free of the confines of that net thing and hung down her back in a long braid, gleaming in the sunlight. He figured her to be about five and a half feet tall, and her slim shape with just the right amount of curves was pleasing to the eye—not his, but probably other men's.

What was that? Lottie singing? He edged closer, careful to not let his rifle clatter against the rocks, certain his ears were deceiving him.

"Amazing Grace"?

Surely not. How could an outlaw be singing a Christian hymn? Brett sat back on his heels, confused to the core. He tugged out the sketch of Lottie and stared at it. There was no doubt in his mind that the woman in the drawing was the same one sitting by the creek bed. *What's going on, Lord?*

Lottie's mare let out a frightened squeal. She pranced and jerked at the tree she was tethered to. The hairs on Brett's nape lifted, and he glanced around to see what had spooked the horse.

From his angle, nothing seemed out of place. Lottie's head jerked up and her singing halted. Suddenly, she jumped off the rock and hurried to her horse. The mare would have bolted if not tied so well.

Brett peered over the boulder to see what was wrong and noticed a cub by the creek. A split second later, a huge grizzly charged out of the brush, angry and roaring.

Without stopping to think, Brett raised his rifle and aimed at the bear's feet. Maybe he could scare it away. Lottie fumbled to free her mare.

If he shot, he'd give himself away and risk not capturing Jack. But he couldn't let Lottie be mauled to death.

He fired until his rifle was empty, and then he jumped off the boulder, between Lottie and the beast. He yanked his pistol free, knowing a bullet from it wouldn't stop a charging bear. He fired at the grizzly's feet, but it didn't even slow down.

The snarling creature lunged at Brett. Its huge teeth glistened with spittle.

Lord, help me.

five

Anna yanked at the reins and murmured soothing sounds to the frightened mare. The horse's frantic jerking at the reins had twisted them into a knot around the low-hanging tree branch. She fought to untangle them, knowing her swift horse would take her to safety. But she only had a few seconds before the bear would be upon her.

The knot wouldn't pull free. Anna's chest tightened as she yanked her Winchester from the scabbard.

Rifle fire and snarling growls sounded behind her. She spun around, her heart turning somersaults. The grizzly lunged at a man Anna had never seen before, swiping him across the chest with her big paw. The creature roared an earsplitting growl in the man's face.

Anna fired two quick shots near the grizzly's hind paws. The huge creature jumped and lurched away from the noise, lumbering back to her cub. The mother thrashed across the creek, and both bears disappeared into the bushes.

Heaving rapid breaths, Anna reloaded and watched to make sure the angry mother didn't return. After a few moments, she dashed to her rescuer's side. If the man hadn't jumped between her and the bear, she'd most likely be dead now.

She quickly tore away the remains of the man's thick coat. At the sight of blood staining his chambray shirt, she winced. *Lord, show me how to help him. Please, save this man's life.*

She untucked her shirt and pulled a small knife from the top of her boot, then cut away as much fabric as she could without exposing herself. Quickly, she unbuttoned the stranger's shirt and gently laid the folded fabric from her own shirt across his

41

wound. Four of the bear's claws had cut tracks into his solid chest, but thanks to his heavy jacket, the injuries didn't look too terribly deep.

He moaned and rolled his head sideways, revealing blood on the flat rock beneath his head. Anna checked his head wound and wished she had something else to use for bandages, but the best thing she could do for this man was to get him home where he could be doctored properly. Looking over her shoulder, she checked to make sure the bear was still gone. They needed to leave before the creature decided to come back to finish her attack. But how could she move a man the size of Quinn all by herself?

He groaned and raised his knees as if trying to stand.

"Mister, can you hear me? We need to get out of here. You've been injured."

His brow wrinkled, and he gritted his teeth. Groaning, he reached for his chest. She grabbed his arm and wrestled it down. Pebbles bit into Anna's knees, but she tried to ignore her pain, knowing it was nothing compared to this man's suffering.

"Who are you?" Had he been watching her? Or did he just happen to be riding by when the bear attacked?

That seemed too much of a coincidence. Anna sucked in a breath. Maybe he was one of the rustlers that Quinn was out hunting.

He tossed his head back and forth, uttering a low growl as if he were still fighting the bear. Anna rushed to the creek and scooped up some water in her hands, then dribbled it into the man's mouth. He coughed but swallowed. Using her hand, she wiped the blood off his dirty cheek. Slowly, as if he'd been in a deep sleep, his eyes opened. He glanced around, confused.

Anna took advantage of his moment of consciousness. "Mister, you've got to get on my horse so I can get you some help."

Lifting hard and wedging her boot behind him, she managed to get him sitting. He cried out and clutched his torso but didn't fight her. Anna's heart stampeded. His life was in her hands.

Please, God, help me get him up.

Anna hurried to Bella, cooing to the still-skittish mare, and untangled the reins, though her hands shook like the leaves of a quaking aspen in a windstorm. She led her horse right up to the man. The mare sniffed at the stranger but stood still. Anna got behind him and hooked her arms under his. "You have to get up. Please. I can't lift you by myself." Surprising her, he struggled to his feet and fell against the horse. Anna strained to keep his heavy body upright. "Can you mount?"

He nodded. It took three tries for him to hook his foot in the stirrup, but with a loud grunt, he finally heaved himself up, holding one arm to his chest. Anna looped the reins over Bella's head and climbed behind the man. With one arm around his solid stomach, holding him tight, she guided Bella home with the other hand.

The short trip took a long while with Bella walking slowly. The stranger hunched over the mare's neck, and Anna couldn't tell if he was conscious or not. As they rode up to the ranch yard, Sam ambled out of the barn. He took one look in her direction and jogged toward them.

"Who you got there, Miss Anna?"

"I don't know, but he saved me from a grizzly attack."

"A grizzly? There ain't been no reports of bear in these parts for a long while."

"Well. . .there is. A bear and her cub."

"Then that makes this feller a friend, I reckon. Where you want 'im?"

"In the house."

Sam took Bella's reins and led the mare toward the cabin.

He looked over his shoulder and yelled, "Hank, get on out here."

The ranch hand ran out of the barn and looked around, then joined them at the stairs. Sam tied Bella to a hitching post, and he and Hank helped Anna get the stranger to the ground. The man would have collapsed if the ranch hands hadn't held him upright. They all but dragged him inside.

"Put him in Adam's room." Anna hurried past them and turned down the bed coverings.

They laid the stranger on the bed, and his feet hung off the end. Sam tugged his boots off and tossed them in a corner. "Who do you suppose he is?"

Anna shrugged. "Don't know, but God must have sent him to save my life."

"Where did you see that bear?" Sam asked.

"Down at the creek." Anna realized how she must look with her shirt half cut off, and she crossed her arms around her middle to try and hide the frayed edges.

"I'll tell Leyna about the man, and then me and Hank'll go after that bear."

"She's got a cub. Don't kill her, just chase her away. All right?"

Sam nodded, and he and Hank left the room. Anna tugged the end of the quilt out from under the stranger's feet and covered them. His wound had bled onto the pillowcase. She hurried to her room, grabbed some towels and the pitcher of fresh water Leyna always supplied, and hurried back to her patient. She met Leyna at the door.

"We have an injured man, *Herr* Sam said."

Anna squeezed past her and set the supplies on Adam's writing desk. She dipped one end of a towel in the water and wiped a trail of blood off the man's temple.

Leyna moved closer and clucked her tongue. "We must stitch him up. I will get the basket of medicines."

Half an hour later, Anna stared at the man. They'd done the best they could to sew up his injuries. Only one had been overly deep, but Leyna had cleaned it well. If infection didn't set in and the man's head wound wasn't too severe, he should recover.

She couldn't help watching the man who'd saved her life. His thick dark brown hair hung over the white bandage on his forehead. Stubble darkened his jaw, giving him a ruggedly handsome look. What color were his eyes? She couldn't remember from the brief moment he'd opened them earlier. What would his voice sound like?

But more importantly, who was he? And why was he on Rocking M land?

Anna closed her eyes. "Heavenly Father, please save this man's life as he did mine. And please heal his wounds. Oh, and please, God, don't let him be a rustler."

❧

Brett struggled to climb his way out of the dark pit. There was a light ahead, and he aimed to reach it. He blinked, then jerked awake, searching for the bear that had attacked him.

"Hey, settle down. You're all right."

A room slowly came into focus. Brett searched for the source of that sweet voice, but a consuming fire burning in his chest demanded his attention. He reached for his chest, needing to douse the flames. Someone yanked his arm back.

"Don't. A bear clawed you. The wounds have been stitched and doctored, and you need to leave them alone."

He turned his head toward the voice, and a woman's pretty features came into view. Her worried, tentative smile twisted his gut.

No. Not Lottie.

"I know you're hurting. I can give you laudanum if the pain is too fierce."

"No." His voice sounded scratchy. Off-kilter. The last thing he needed was to let Lottie Sallinger drug him, no matter how bad the pain was.

But, oh goodness, did she smell good. Up close, she was even prettier—and her eyes were brown, the color of coffee without cream. Beautiful. He must be delirious.

"Could you drink some water?"

That angelic voice couldn't belong to an outlaw. Brett nodded and struggled to sit up. His chest felt as if a giant fist had seized him and wouldn't let go, and he was sure his head had landed between a blacksmith's hammer and anvil.

"Careful, now. You don't want to bust out those stitches." Lottie reached behind him and helped to guide him up just enough to drink. He guzzled the cool liquid until she took it away.

"That's enough for now."

Brett lay back, trying to catch his breath. He hated being at the mercy of outlaws, no matter how nice they treated him. He knew the truth. Still, how could this sweet, gentle woman be the same gal who robbed a bank? He must have hit his head hard when that bear plowed into him.

"My name is Anna McFarland. You're on the Rocking M Ranch. What's your name?"

An angel with golden hair smiled at him. If not for the pain, he'd think he'd died and gone to heaven. But Taylor wasn't here, so he couldn't be in heaven.

No, he was in the lair of his enemy.

"You got a name?"

He licked his dry lips. "Brett." That was all she needed to know for now.

"Well, Mr. Brett, I don't know how to thank you for coming to my aid like you did. You most likely saved my life." Lottie twisted her hands, and a becoming pink shade stained her cheeks.

"You're welcome, and it's just Brett. No mister." He might

have to arrest her, but he was glad that snarly old bear hadn't damaged Lottie's beautiful skin. Was it as soft as it looked?

Brett turned away and pursed his lips. He had no business thinking such things. He chalked it up to the weakness of the moment. A skillfully drawn picture of a herd of cattle on a peaceful hillside snagged his attention. Whoever had drawn that was very talented. On the wall opposite the bed, there hung a drawing of a pretty woman dressed in a flannel shirt, a split riding skirt, and boots. A western hat tilted on the side of her head gave the woman a cocky air.

"That's my sister-in-law, Mariah. My brother Adam drew all these sketches."

"He's very good."

Lottie nodded. "Yes, he is. He's traveling the West with his wife. He sketches Western scenes for a Chicago gallery owner who frames and sells them. His wife writes dime novels."

Brett's gaze darted to Lottie's. "A woman writer?"

Lottie's warm smile tempted him to believe she was a good, wholesome woman. "Mariah is quite successful at writing dime novels. Maybe you'd like to read some when you're feeling better."

Brett grunted, neither a yes or no. He didn't want to become any more beholden to the Sallingers.

Lottie rose. "You should rest. Is there anything you need first?"

He shook his head, instantly wishing he hadn't.

"Are you sure you don't want some laudanum?" She stood and gazed at him with concerned eyes.

"No. I'm sure." He needed a clear head.

"Well. . .if you change your mind, just let me know. I'll check on you in a little while."

Brett knew he should thank her, but the words tasted bitter on his tongue. How had he gotten himself in this predicament?

He glanced at and lifted the sheet, taking small breaths

to avoid the pain larger ones caused. His torso resembled a mummy with that white bandage wrapped all around him. He wanted to check out his injuries, but he didn't want to mess up the bandage. He'd just have to wait until they changed it.

The bedroom was small but nicely furnished with a double bed, desk and chair, a small wardrobe, and a wingback chair in the corner. A pale blue curtain fluttered on the breeze coming in the partially open window. The scent of cattle drifted in, mixed with the fragrant odor of something cooking. His stomach grumbled.

His gaze traveled to the ceiling. "Well, Lord, I'm in a fine mess, aren't I? Thank you for protecting me—and Lottie—from that bear."

Now what? Would Jack recognize him for the lawman he was? His badge!

Brett hunted for his shirt and found it hanging on the bedpost. He reached for it with his left hand, gritting his teeth against the burning pain in his chest, and searched the tattered remains of his shirt for his U.S. Marshal's badge. Where was it? Had Lottie already found it and kept it to show her brother?

He was wearing it before the attack, wasn't he? Brett stopped to remember what happened just before the bear charged. He'd put on his fleece coat because lying on the stony ground had hurt his belly. The jacket offered some protection, even if it made him sweat.

Maybe the bear had knocked his badge off. Ignoring the pain any movement caused, he checked his pants pockets. No badge, but there was a piece of paper. He pulled out the sketch of Lottie and glanced toward the open door. He quickly unfolded the single sheet. Anna McFarland was a dead ringer for Lottie Sallinger—and he'd just wormed his way into her hideout.

six

Anna hummed as she arranged the breakfast items on the plate for her patient.

"That stranger, he is handsome, ja?" Leyna glanced sideways at Anna as she rolled balls of dough, her green eyes twinkling with mischief.

To disagree would be telling a falsehood, but she wouldn't play Leyna's game. "Yes, he is a nice-looking man. I think he's even taller than Quinn."

"*Herr* Quinn, he will not like that you have brought a stranger into the house with him gone."

Anna spun around toward the cook. "Why not? That man saved my life. I couldn't very well leave him to die."

"*Ach.* He should be in the bunkhouse with the other men."

"Well, he's not. It would be too hard to take care of him." Anna yanked up the tray, sloshing coffee onto the saucer. Maybe it wasn't the wisest thing, bringing a stranger into the house with her brother gone, but she hadn't stopped to think about that yesterday. All she'd wanted was to get the man's wounds treated so he wouldn't die. She couldn't bear it if that happened after he saved her life.

She peeked past the open door to see if Brett was awake. He lay sprawled out on top of the bed, one hand behind his head. Clean, white bandages swaddled his torso, making his dusty pants stand out. What would he say when he noticed what they'd done to him?

She couldn't tell if he was sleeping or just looking out the window. The tray clunked as she set it on the desk. Brett turned his sleepy gaze on her, and her breath caught in her

49

throat. With his hair tousled and a relaxed look in his eyes, instead of that wary, on-guard stare he'd worn the day before, he was quite handsome. He rubbed his whiskers and gave her a lazy smile. *Oh my!* Anna dropped into the chair before her legs could give out.

"Something sure smells good. What do you have there? I'm as hungry as a bear." Brett glanced down at his body, then reached to his right and grabbed the sheet, throwing it over him.

Anna shook her head at his bear reference and cleared her throat. "Oh, just eggs, bacon, and biscuits."

He pushed himself up in the bed, wincing.

"Are you in much pain?"

The dark look returned, as if he didn't like being reminded of his current situation. "I'm fine."

Anna handed him a pillow, which he placed across his lap; then she set the tray on top of it. "Sorry, I spilled the coffee."

"Not a problem." He lifted the cup and slurped the coffee from the saucer, then sipped from the cup. "Mmm. . .hot and black, just how I like it."

He tossed her a hesitant glance, bowed his head for a moment, and then dug into his food as if he hadn't eaten in a week. Was he praying? If the man was a Christian, that would certainly calm Leyna's nerves about having him in the house.

His ever-changing expressions confused Anna. One minute he looked like an outlaw with his two-day stubble and his deep blue eyes narrowed in a glare; then he'd lighten up and flash an ornery smile that made her feel as if moths were fluttering in her stomach.

The question still remained. . .who was he?

"Very good food. Thank the cook, would you?"

Anna nodded. "I'll do that. Um. . .I've been wondering. . . how was it you just happened to be right there when that bear charged out of the brush?"

He shrugged one shoulder. "Fortunate timing, I suppose."

"Yes, it was that. But that still doesn't explain why you were on the Rocking M."

Anna hiked her chin up, showing him she meant business.

"I heard in town that this was a good place to find work." He laid his hand on his chest. "Guess I won't be much good for work for a while, though."

"Don't worry about that. You just concentrate on healing. I'm sure my brother would be happy to hire you once you're better."

Instead of looking happy about that, he scowled and stared out the window. Maybe he didn't like not pulling his own weight. Though rarely sick, Quinn hated being in bed and not able to work. Maybe Brett felt the same way.

"There's not a lot you can do right now. Would you mind if I read to you?"

He shook his head. "No, I don't mind."

"Wonderful. Let me grab something to read, and I'll be right back." The chair creaked as she stood. Could this stranger be an answer to her prayer? Caring for him definitely gave her something to do. At least for now.

❧

Brett wanted to throw something. Never had he been in such a frustrating situation. Accepting food and medical care from the very people who'd killed his brother didn't sit right with him. His grip tightened on the sheet covering him. He felt the need to flee in the night and put some distance between himself and the Sallingers, but at the same time, it seemed as if God had plunked him right in the middle of that nest of vipers. Besides, even if he wanted to leave, he would have to wait another day or two until he healed more. He could barely move without his chest burning with pain, and his ribs ached from the bear's heavy weight landing on him.

And where was Jasper? Was he still tied to a juniper shrub or had Lottie found his gelding and brought him back here?

The time right after the bear attack was still foggy in his mind.

She reentered the room with a thick leather book under her arm. He sure hoped she didn't plan to read that whole thing to him. She situated herself in the soft chair in the corner and opened the tome. A Bible?

Brett narrowed his gaze. What was going on here? Was this a ruse to throw him off the trail? Were the Sallingers people who justified their deeds by misrepresenting God's Word?

"Ready for me to read to you?" Lottie's engaging smile withered under his stern scowl.

It was best he listen carefully to see if she tried to manipulate the scriptures for her own purposes. A Bible-reading bank robber. . .he'd seen everything now.

She cleared her throat. "Blessed is the man that walketh not in the counsel of the ungodly, nor standeth in the way of sinners, nor sitteth in the seat of the scornful. But his delight is in the law of the Lord; and in his law doth he meditate day and night. And he shall be like a tree planted by the rivers of water, that bringeth forth his fruit in his season; his leaf also shall not wither; and whatsoever he doeth shall prosper. The ungodly are not so: but are like the chaff which the wind driveth away."

Brett's mouth dropped open as Lottie's sweet voice softly read the words from Psalm 1. He scratched at the bandage around his head, trying to make sense of it all. Maybe that bump on his head had rendered him unconscious and this was nothing but a dream. Or maybe his mind had been knocked off-kilter and he was crazy now.

There had to be some mistake. Either this wasn't Lottie or some woman other than Lottie had robbed the bank. But the sketch he'd gotten from Marshal Cronan had been drawn on the day of the robbery, while the bank clerk's mind was still fresh and clear.

The only other possibility was that the clerk had described someone other than Lottie—maybe a patron at the bank? There had been a lot of confusion with Taylor's shooting and that bag of coins getting dropped just outside on the boardwalk. Was it possible the clerk had described the wrong person?

As he listened to the scripture, his hands ached to pull out the sketch and compare it to Lottie. She read for a solid half hour, and Brett gave up wrestling the facts and let God's Word minister to him. God had a plan, even in this odd situation he'd found himself in.

Something clanked at the doorway, and he and Lottie both looked up. The older woman he remembered from yesterday entered, carrying a basin holding bandages and some kind of salve.

"*Guten morgen.* How is our patient this day?" She smiled and set the basin on the foot of the bed.

"He ate well, Leyna."

"Good! You like my cooking, ja?"

Brett couldn't help returning the German woman's warm smile. "Ja."

Leyna chuckled. "You won't like so well the doctoring."

Brett laid his hand on his chest and glanced at Lottie. Maybe it was silly, but the bandage covered him so well that he hadn't thought about being shirtless in her presence, but now. . .

"You must sit up so we can unwrap the binding; then I will tend your wounds."

Trying to ignore the fact that Lottie was still in the room, Brett did as the cook ordered, hissing against the pain as he sat up. He focused his attention on the cook. Was she one of the many Russian Germans who'd come to North Dakota looking for land and freedom? How had she gotten hooked up with outlaws? Was she even aware the Sallingers were thieves and murderers?

With the binding off, Leyna gently pushed him back down

and carefully peeled off the bandages covering the wounds. Brett clenched his jaw. That old bear had made tracks on his chest, and with all those stitches and red welts, he looked like a scarecrow. He was lucky to be alive. Narrowing his gaze, he realized something was wrong. He sucked in a breath and looked up. "You shaved my chest?"

Lottie winced at his booming voice, but Leyna only tsk-tsked. "Hush your bellowing. It was necessary to avoid infection."

Brett started to rub a hand over the chest that hadn't been bald since he was seventeen, but Leyna smacked it away. He felt. . .violated somehow, which was silly since he knew the hair would grow back. At least he hoped it would. Leyna made quick work of her doctoring, and he lay back, more tired than he wanted to admit. Lottie handed her the salve and clean bandages, watching him with a worried stare.

"I will get you one of *Herr* Quinn's shirts to wear." Leyna left as quickly as she'd come.

Lottie hugged the Bible to her chest. "Would you like me to read some more?"

He dreaded the thought of wearing one of Jack Sallinger's shirts and just wanted them to leave him alone. He shook his head. Lottie stood by the bed, looking disappointed. Guilt needled Brett.

The last thing he wanted was to feel sympathy for the Sallingers, no matter how nice they had been to him. He was a lawman, and they were outlaws. He supposed even outlaws had some good in them. That was evident. But he couldn't afford to be swayed into lowering his defenses. Just as soon as he got the evidence he needed, Lottie and her brother were going to jail for a very long time.

He turned onto his side, almost grateful for the pain. The clomping of boots sounded in the next room and stopped at the bedroom doorway.

"Quinn! You're back."

Brett carefully rolled onto his back and saw Lottie hugging a man. He lightly patted her shoulder then pushed her away and glared at Brett.

"Just what's going on here? And why aren't you still in Bismarck?" He directed the last question at Lottie.

Up close, Jack Sallinger was taller and broader than Brett had expected. His blond hair and brown eyes favored his sister's, though Lottie's hair was more a golden blond, and she was much shorter than her brother. There was no denying the affection between the two, but Jack seemed more interested in Brett than his sister.

"This is Brett. He saved my life." Lottie's warm smile of gratitude made Brett want to slink under his covers and hide.

"Yeah, the men told me what happened." His hard expression softened. "I owe you my thanks, Mister. You got a last name?"

Brett couldn't abide lying, so he would just have to give his real name and hope Jack hadn't heard of him. "Wickham, Brett Wickham."

Jack nodded. "What are you doing in these parts? It's a long ways from nowhere."

"I heard you might be hiring." That was true. Hadn't the man at the café in Medora said the Rocking M might be hiring?

"I can always use another good hand. You done any ranching?"

Brett grinned. "Yep. Plenty. My pa owned a ranch down south a ways." He held the grin in place, even as thoughts of Taylor's limp body saturated his mind. The Bar W now belonged to Brett alone, and he would need to return soon. But first, he'd see the Sallingers behind bars.

"Well. . .you rest up and let the ladies coddle you for a few days. Then I'll put you to work." Jack smirked, making Brett wonder if there was more to his words than the obvious. "Thanks for coming to my sister's rescue. I'm much obliged."

Jack stormed out of the room as fast as he'd come. Lottie cast him a hesitant glance and followed her brother. Brett lay back. God had placed him right smack in his enemies' lair. Now all he needed was to find evidence to convict the two.

❧

"He's hiding something." Quinn stopped in front of the parlor window. He turned and scowled at Anna. "How could you bring a stranger into this house when I was gone? That's just plain dumb, Anna."

She crossed her arms and mentally prepared to defend her stance again. "He was hurt bad. I didn't stop to think. The man had saved me from a horrible death or maiming, most likely, and all I wanted was to get him some help."

She wanted to protect her champion, but she couldn't let her brother's concern slide past. "Why do you think he's hiding something?"

"Just a feeling I have. It's too coincidental that he was right there when you needed him."

"Maybe God sent him." She lifted her brows, daring him to argue that fact.

He heaved a sigh. Standing there with his hands on his hips as he glared down might intimidate their ranch hands, but not her.

"Maybe so, but I'm still suspicious. Sam found a horse on the butte overlooking the creek."

"And?" Anna prayed Brett wasn't a rustler. *Please, Lord.*

Quinn turned up one side of his mouth. "Nothing. He just had some food supplies, a change of clothes, and some ammunition. Nothing to show who he was or why he was on our land. Sam thinks he may have been watching you."

Anna's eyes widened and her heart leaped in her chest. "Why?"

Quinn shrugged. "Maybe he's one of the rustlers and was keeping an eye on you. Maybe he's just a man watching a pretty woman."

If Anna hadn't been so concerned, she was certain she

would have blushed at her brother's rare compliment. Had Brett been watching her? Just the thought sent chills up and down her spine.

"As soon as he can get around, I want him out in the bunkhouse where the other men can help keep an eye on him. That man is up to something. You stay out of Adam's room and let Leyna tend him."

Anna wanted to say he was making a mountain out of a molehill, but one had to be cautious in this wilderness they lived in. Still, Brett intrigued her like no man ever had.

Was it because he'd charged in like a medieval knight, risking his own life to save her?

Quinn could move Brett to the barn, but until the man was gone, he was still her patient. . .and tend him, she would.

seven

Anna glanced at her reflection in the mirror on the wardrobe's door, admiring the fine job Leyna had done fashioning the emerald fabric she'd purchased in Bismarck into a lovely dress. Her mother had planned to make her something from the fabric, but somehow the material had gotten placed in the supplies Anna had brought home. She glanced down at the hem she had stitched herself and pressed her lips together. Was that a pucker?

Oh well, with the skirt as full as it was, who would notice anyway? She searched the wardrobe and found her beaded reticule in a drawer. She hadn't used it since her trip to Bismarck and didn't remember the bag being so heavy. Pulling open the drawstring, she dumped the contents onto her bed. Anna gasped at the two shiny gold coins resting on her quilt. Two double-eagle coins stared at her, sending stabbing shards of guilt throughout her. She felt as guilty as if she'd robbed that bank herself. The coins must have somehow fallen into her bag during the bank robbery.

What now?

Just touching money that didn't belong to her made her feel dirty. Could she be arrested for being in possession of stolen money? *Heavenly Father, what should I do?*

Who would believe that the coins had fallen into her reticule by accident? The bank officials would most likely accuse her of stealing them—at least that skinny bank clerk would.

Anna searched for a place to hide the coins until she could figure out how to get them back to the bank. If she just walked in and tried to return them, that bank clerk might implicate her in the robbery. No, she'd just have to find another way. They were far too heavy to mail. Maybe she could mail forty dollars paper money back to the bank.

Anna rifled through her drawers, finally deciding to hide the coins beneath her underwear. Nobody would dare get in that drawer except Leyna, and she would believe Anna's story of how the coins came into her possession. Should she tell Quinn? The bank clerk's accusations rang in her ears. No, it was best she find a way to return the money herself.

Quickly, she stuffed her belongings back into her reticule, affixed her hat, and hurried out to find Quinn. He'd promised to take her to town to hear the circuit-riding minister this Sunday. When she didn't find him in the parlor, she searched the kitchen. Leyna sat at the table, sipping coffee, her face pale.

"What's wrong? Has something happened?"

The cook waved her hand in the air. "*Herr* Quinn, he rode out early this morning. One of the hands, he found a dead cow."

Anna's heart sunk. "So he's not taking us to church?"

Leyna shook her head, but a smile tugged at her lips. "I will not go today. My head, it feels like a horse sat on it. But *Herr* Quinn says that *Herr* Brett will drive you."

Anna perked up at this news. "Truly?"

Leyna nodded, then grimaced. "*Ja*, it is the truth."

Her joy quickly turned to concern. "But is he ready for that? He's barely been out of bed the past three days since the attack."

"*Herr* Quinn is anxious to have him out of the house." The cook waved at the stove. "The stew, I will put it on for your dinner, then go back to *mein* bed."

Anna clasped the cook's arm. "No, you go to bed now. I can fix something when I return if there isn't a picnic after the service. Do I need to bring back the doctor?"

"*Nein.*" When Leyna didn't argue about cooking dinner,

Anna knew she must be feeling poorly. Anna nibbled her lip as Leyna pushed up from the chair.

"I could stay home and take care of you."

"*Nein.* You go. I just sleep. But *danke.*" A feeble smile touched Leyna's lips as she walked out of the room. The older woman was hale and hardy and rarely ever sick. Anna prayed she would feel better soon.

Outside on the porch, Anna searched for Brett. It was too soon for him to be driving a wagon to town and back. What was Quinn thinking?

She'd just find Brett and tell him that she was quite capable of driving the rig herself. Before she could take a step, a horse and buggy came out of the barn. Brett guided it right up to the porch and stopped.

"Whoa."

He tipped his hat and smiled, sending Anna's stomach into spasms. Why did he have to be so fine looking?

He stood and started to climb down.

"No!"

His brows lifted, and he halted at Anna's stern command.

Her cheeks turned crimson. "I mean, save your strength. You don't need to get down and help me up. I've been climbing into buggies since I could walk."

He nodded then reached out a hand to help her up. She stared at it, afraid he'd break loose his stitches if he did too much.

"Take my hand. . .Miss McFarland."

"I don't want to hurt you." Ignoring his hand, she climbed up beside him and arranged her skirts. He picked up the reins with a sigh and clicked out the side of his mouth to the horse. The buggy lurched and started forward.

Anna had to admit that in the light of day Brett looked healthier, less pale. He'd shaved this morning, revealing his strong jaw. Seeing him up and moving about sent a shaft of relief charging through her. If he had died saving her, she would have borne that pain her whole life. Brett was a fine-looking man, broad-shouldered and tall, and those eyes. . .

Oh, bother! What was she doing admiring a man who might well be an outlaw?

He glanced out the corner of his eye at her and smiled. The buggy dipped, and his shoulder brushed against hers. She turned away, ignoring what that smile and his touch—albeit accidental—did to her insides, and studied the landscape. Soon all the green would turn to brown stubble and the temperature would grow too cold for a two-hour trip to Medora for church—or anything else. She'd be stuck at the ranch for another winter. It had never really bothered her until Adam had left. What would she do cooped up for months on end?

"Nice day to go to church."

Anna turned to Brett. "You go to church often?" Maybe she could trap him into revealing his true purpose for being on the Rocking M.

"Yep. Every chance I get. There are too many troubles in this world. A man needs to be reminded of God's grace and love."

He pressed his lips together and looked away. What troubles was he talking about? Would a rustler go to church? If Quinn still suspected him, he'd never allow Brett to escort her, so that must mean her brother was satisfied that Brett wasn't a threat to them.

No, surely he wasn't a rustler. If he were, he would have been on edge in their home and not so relaxed. Brett confused her more than any man she'd met. And the trouble was. . .she liked him. More than liked him, she was attracted to him.

A church-going man couldn't be a rustler. That was all there was to it, and that's what she'd choose to believe.

❧

Guilt surged through Brett. He'd all but told Lottie a lie, and that didn't sit well with him. Sunday service was the last place he wanted to go today. He hadn't yet made peace with God for his brother's death. But he had to see for himself that Lottie was going to church or he would never believe it possible.

His own words needled him. *A man needs to be reminded of God's grace and love.* Where had they come from? Was it a message from God to him, straight out of his own mouth?

For three days he'd lain in bed, stewing over Taylor's death. He knew God would comfort him if Brett would allow it, but he'd clung to his anger like a child clinging to a broken toy. How else could he keep his distance from Lottie and her constant, sweet ministration?

Jack Sallinger hadn't been happy to find Brett in his house. Lottie's brother was suspicious of him, which was only natural, especially with his sister tending to a stranger. Jack had shaved and looked little like the verbal description he had received from Marshal Cronan, but things had happened so fast at the bank. How much could he count on the eyewitnesses who'd been in fear of their lives? Most folks in such a situation would avoid looking a robber in the face.

The wagon dipped in a rut, knocking Lottie's shoulder against his again. The fresh scent of something floral wafted in the air. His gut tightened. He didn't want to be attracted to her. Sure, she was a beautiful woman, but she was an outlaw. Remember Taylor? Remember all that stolen money?

Brett hated how his own mind and body threatened to betray his brother's memory. He couldn't allow his defenses to be broken down just because Lottie doted on him and fed him—great food—and read the Bible to him. *God, help me. I don't want to like the Sallingers.*

"May I ask you a question?" Lottie peeked sideways at him.

His heart skittered. What did she want to know? How could he answer without lying and giving himself away? "Sure," he said, against his better judgment.

"Where are you from?"

Ah, that he could answer. "I grew up on a ranch south of here a ways."

"Why would you want to work for us if your family owns a ranch?" She turned curious, innocent eyes toward him.

He blinked. How could a thieving, gun-toting outlaw look so guileless? "Ah. . .my pa was quite strict. I left there over five years ago."

Lottie nodded. "Our pa was strict, too, but he died a long time ago. I think that's why Quinn is like he is."

"Like what?"

She shrugged. "I don't know. He works all the time. He's been the closest thing to a father Adam and I have had since Pa's death, but he's never been affectionate—has always held himself away from us for some reason."

"Maybe he's afraid of losing someone else he loves."

Lottie looked at him with wide brown eyes, as if she'd never considered that notion. "You might be right. I hadn't ever thought of that. Our ranch in Texas wasn't doing very well after several years of drought, so Pa came up north, bought the Rocking M, and moved us here."

Brett held the reins loosely and watched a hawk circling in the bright blue sky. After three days of being shut up in that bedroom, he enjoyed the sun's warmth. Something pricked at the back of his mind. . .if the McFarlands were wealthy enough to buy all this land, why would they risk it and their nice home to rob trains and banks? Something else that didn't fit the picture. "That was a long move. Must have been hard."

"Actually"—Lottie glanced at him, her eyes dancing—"I thought it was a big adventure. But I did miss my friends from school, and I felt sorry for Adam when his horse died. He was sad for so long after that."

The gentle rocking of the buggy and warmth of the sun lulled Brett into a relaxed state. He yawned and stretched, instantly sorry. He sucked in a breath and rubbed his chest. Lottie cast him a worried glance.

"I can drive if you're in pain."

"No. Just remind me not to stretch again."

Lottie's laugh kindled an awareness inside him that he didn't want fueled.

"Sorry, I shouldn't find humor in your pain."

Brett didn't respond. He tightened his grasp on the reins and clenched his teeth. He couldn't afford to like Lottie Sallinger—but those brown sugar eyes made him want to believe she was as innocent as she seemed.

A half hour later, they pulled up to the church. The singing had already started. Brett escorted Lottie to a seat in back, then tended the horse and returned. He was thankful they were in the last row so that no one could see him squirm. Vengeance wasn't right in the eyes of God; he knew that. Could he dispense justice without being overcome with vengeance? Would it be right to leave now and go home to the Bar W and let the Sallingers run free to wreak havoc on other innocent folks?

"Vengeance is mine, saith the Lord." The minister shouted the words and smacked his Bible on the makeshift pulpit. Brett jumped, and Lottie stared at him with wide eyes. She pressed her lips together as if holding in a smile, but it broke forth, dancing in her eyes. As she turned back to face the preacher, a grin twittered on her enticing lips.

He glanced around to see if anyone else had noticed his discomfort, but all eyes were pinned on the man up front. Brett settled in to listen, wondering how the minister had picked that of all messages to preach this day.

"Man seeks to avenge the wrong done him, but God's Word says to leave vengeance to Him. Anger and hatred drives man away from God. Satan feeds that anger until it becomes a raging fire that man can't put out on his own. God asks us to lay aside our anger and let Him deal with those who have wronged us."

Brett hung his head. If he turned things over to God, it would seem as if he deserted his brother. Exacting justice was his job as a lawman. How could he just go home and do nothing?

The service complete, people filed outside, shaking the preacher's hand as they passed him. Women set about pulling pots and platters of food from their wagons and putting them on makeshift tables the men had put up. Lottie nibbled her lip and walked over to him.

"We didn't bring any food. I feel funny eating when I didn't bring anything."

"Let's go then." Brett reached for her arm, just as a burly man stepped onto the bed of a nearby wagon.

"I know some of you folks live a ways out of town and didn't get word about our picnic today, but there's plenty of food, so we invite you to stay and eat."

The crowd erupted in a chorus of affirmation. Lottie shrugged. "Well. . .do you feel up to staying and eating?"

The minister's words still niggled at Brett. Letting go of his quest for vengeance was the right thing to do, but he just didn't know how to release it. He wanted to hit the road, but if he started working at the Rocking M, he wouldn't get to town very often. Maybe he should take advantage of the chance to nose around and see what he could find out about the McFarlands. "Sure, I can always eat."

Brett wolfed down his food and went to check on the horse. The curious glances Lottie's unmarried women friends sent his way set his nerves on edge. He felt like a worm on a hook, dangling over a lake with a dozen widemouthed bass ready to take a bite out of him.

He checked the mare and then led her over to the water trough. Another man, short and thin, was already watering a fine-looking bay mare. Brett nodded to him. "Afternoon."

The man smiled. "Name's John Cutter. Saw you in church with Anna McFarland. You her new beau?"

Brett sniffed a laugh. Him? Lottie Sallinger's beau? That would be the day. "Uh. . .no, I'm just escorting her at her brother's orders. I work on the Rocking M."

"Lucky you, getting a peek at Anna McFarland every day. Most of the unmarried men in Medora would like to court her, but that brother of hers chases them all away." The man glanced past the crowd to where Lottie stood beneath a pine tree, chatting with two men.

Brett followed his gaze, his hand tightening on the reins as one of the men leaned in close to Lottie and said something. She lifted her hand to her mouth and stepped back, looking uncomfortable with the man's attention. Her gaze darted past the men, scanning the crowd. Was she looking for him?

Brett tied the mare to a tree where there was still some green grass in reach and let her graze. A desire to protect Lottie forced his feet forward. He strode toward her, wondering about his feelings. Was he actually jealous? Or did he just want to take good care of his charge? Jack had told him to guard his sister with his life. Brett huffed a laugh. He'd already done that once and had the scars to prove it, not to mention a bald chest.

The rocky ground crunched beneath his feet as he made up the distance in quick order. Was that relief in Lottie's gaze when she noticed him?

&

Anna watched Brett storm toward her. What had put a burr under his saddle?

Still, she couldn't help being relieved at his presence. Spenser Gilroy and Tommy Baxter had cornered her and wouldn't leave her be. How could she have ever considered either of them marrying material? As soon as she returned home, she'd scratch both names off her potential husband list.

Brett moved to her side, staring down the two shorter men. She introduced the three men, noting the scowls on Spenser's and Tommy's faces when she took Brett's arm. If he was surprised, he didn't react.

"You ready to leave yet?" He looked down at her.

"Yes, thank you." She said her good-byes and allowed Brett to escort her toward the buggy, wondering at the tingles charging up her arm where it touched his.

Arm in arm, Pamela, Paula, and Phyllis Stewart intercepted them before they could escape. The three red-haired, stair-step sisters in their late teens giggled and looked at Brett as if he were their Christmas present all wrapped up with a pretty bow. He stopped three yards in front of their unified barricade.

"Aren't you going to introduce us to your *friend*, Anna?" Phyllis patted her hair, pulled so tightly into a bun that Anna wondered why her eyes weren't slanted upward.

"This is Brett Wickham. He's working on the ranch." She wanted to cling to Brett's arm just to watch their response but turned loose of him instead.

"Ladies." He tipped his hat then turned to her. "I'll hitch up the buggy. It will be ready whenever you are."

The big chicken strode away, his long legs eating up the ground. Anna nearly giggled at his hasty escape.

"Oh, my." Paula fanned herself as she watched him depart.

Pamela turned back to Anna. "Where did you find him? He's absolutely delicious."

"And a church-goin' man, too." Phyllis hugged her Bible to her chest.

"He saved me from a bear." Anna held back a smile as three sets of hazel eyes widened in unison.

Pamela puckered her lips in a smirk. "Anna McFarland, that is a falsehood. There's no bear in these parts."

Anna hiked up her chin. "It's true. I promise. I was down at the creek a short ways from our cabin when I saw a cub come out of the brush. I knew the mama bear would be nearby and tried to leave, but Bella's reins had gotten tangled and I couldn't get them untied. If Brett hadn't shown up when he did, that bear most likely would have killed me."

"*Ohh*. . .that's the most romantic thing I've ever heard." Paula fanned herself and peered over her shoulder at Brett.

"He's not married, is he?" Phyllis turned completely around, watching him.

Brett glanced their way then turned his back and busied himself with hitching the horse to the buggy. Anna wasn't sure, but she thought he might be blushing. "I've had a lovely time today, but we must be heading back. The bear clawed Brett across the chest, and I imagine he's getting tired. This is his first day up and about."

The three girls gasped. Anna sidled past them, feeling more than a little proud that she was the one leaving with Brett. She didn't know all that much about him, but she liked him anyway and thought they had become friends. He did save her life, and she his. Just as long as he didn't turn out to be a rustler, everything would be fine.

Maybe she should add his name to the top of her prospective husband list. *Hmm.* Anna Wickham had a nice sound to it.

eight

Anna looked out the parlor window, hoping for a peek at Brett. She'd only seen him a little yesterday, after returning from church. Quinn had assigned him light chores to do today, and he'd been outside since breakfast, when Quinn had told him it was time he moved to the bunkhouse.

Her brother strode out of the barn and soon entered the house. His gray cotton shirt had a long tear in it, and he walked by, not even noticing her. A line of dirt ran down his right cheek.

"What happened?"

He halted suddenly and spun around, squinting at her. "Didn't see you there." He peered down at his chest. "I was checking a cut on a calf's leg, and she got cantankerous. Her hoof got snagged on my pocket and tore my shirt."

"You're not hurt?"

"No."

"That's good. I need to go into town."

He scowled at her swift topic change and unbuttoned his shirt. "I can't take you today. Besides, you were just there yesterday."

"But the stores are closed on Sunday." Anna stepped toward him.

Quinn sidestepped around her and headed toward his room. He quickly changed his shirt and scowled at her as he tucked it into his jeans. Her brother was a fine-looking man. At twenty-seven, he should have been married and fathered several children by now, but he'd put his life on hold to make the ranch the success it was, so they'd all have a nice home.

69

Did he ever regret working so hard? Not taking any time for himself?

"You just bought a wagonload of supplies in Bismarck, sis. What else could you possibly need?"

Anna lifted her chin. "I want to make a quilt."

Quinn opened his mouth and shut it, probably shocked that she now desired to do something she'd always resisted before. "Well. . .uh, that's great news, but doesn't Leyna have enough scraps around here for that?"

If Anna was going to go to all the work and time to make a quilt, she wanted one that would last and look pretty, not one made of scraps. "If I buy new fabric for the quilt, it will last much longer."

Quinn sighed. "All right. Sam's not too busy. He can take you."

"Umm. . .what's Brett doing today?" Anna held her hands in front of her, hoping Quinn wouldn't know she was attracted to their new hand.

Her brother's brows dipped down. "Repairing and polishing tack. Why?"

"Oh, I just thought maybe he could take me since there's not a whole lot he can do yet."

"He's not your personal worker. I've assigned him chores to do."

Anna hiked her chin. "Fine. Then I'll just ride Bella and go alone."

Quinn shook his head and headed down the hall. "I'll have Brett hitch up the buggy."

Anna smiled. She would have preferred riding Bella, because the ride would be smoother and the trip would have taken less time, but this way, she could spend a good four hours with Brett. Maybe she could learn more about him.

❧

As Brett drove the buggy out of Medora, Anna smiled to herself. Her timing had been impeccable. The train had come this morning and brought with it a dozen bolts of new fabric for the mercantile, which was normally low on such items. The indigo, rose, and jade fabric she'd picked out would make a beautiful quilt to decorate her bed. She just hoped that sewing would be easier than the last time she'd tried it. Her fingers had been sore for a week and had resembled a pincushion with all the pricks they'd borne.

Though sewing was one of her least favorite things to do, she'd resigned herself to making a quilt. When Brett wasn't watching, she'd asked the store clerk about work in town. He'd been surprised by her inquiry but had directed her to a wall in the back where notices were posted. While there were notices for cowhands, a farrier, and a man to work in the livery, there wasn't a single position for a woman. It didn't seem fair, but that's the way it was. Women were stuck at home while men got to do all the interesting things.

She peeked at Brett. He hadn't talked much on the trip to town, and she wondered if he was angry with her for taking him away from the harness repair Quinn had assigned him to. "That was a tasty lunch we had in the café, wasn't it? I particularly liked that apple cake. Mmm..."

He nodded but kept his gaze focused on the road ahead. Anna sighed and sat back. How was a woman supposed to get to know a man when he seemed determined not to talk?

"Tell me more about your parents' ranch." She swatted at a fly buzzing her face.

"There's not much to tell. It's just a ranch. We raise several breeds of cattle, grow some hay, have a garden."

"Do you have any brothers or sisters?"

When Brett didn't answer, Anna glanced at his face. His brows dipped down, and his lips were pressed tightly together. He breathed heavily through his nose. Why would such a simple question cause such a reaction? Had he lost a sibling? Her curiosity took her mind in different directions, but she kept her mouth shut, afraid she might say the wrong thing.

Just outside of town, they passed a trail that Anna had never explored before. She'd never had cause to ride up it, but she couldn't help wondering what was around that bend in the trail. If she'd been on Bella, she just might have satisfied her curiosity.

Deciding Brett wasn't going to answer her, she sighed and stared forward, thinking about what design she wanted to use for her quilt. On the butte overlooking the trail, she noticed three elk grazing. The majestic male had a rack that looked as large as a tree branch. He lifted his head and sniffed.

A loud scream rent the serene setting. Anna jumped. Brett yanked back on the reins to keep the spooked horse from bolting. He locked the brake, wrapped the reins around it, and grabbed his rifle.

Anna scooted closer to him and turned her head toward the sound. "What was that?"

"Don't know. Some kind of cat maybe." He stood and jumped off the buggy. "I'll check it out. You stay here and calm the horse."

His boots crunched on the rocky ground as he walked away. Anna descended from the buggy. There was no way she was staying behind when he had the only rifle. She glanced at the horse, which had already settled, and quickly tied it to a cottonwood trunk. Tiptoeing, she hurried to catch up with Brett.

He glanced over his shoulder and scowled. "You don't obey very well."

The eerie cry came again. Closer this time. Anna shivered and grabbed the back of Brett's shirt. He tiptoed forward, his rifle ready.

They heard a clunking sound, and Brett stopped just past the boulder that shielded them. Anna peeked around his arm, still clinging to him. She wasn't generally frightened easily, but that had been such a strange, creepy sound.

Another high-pitched shriek split the air just as she rounded the corner. A dirty, shabbily dressed girl with dingy hair jumped up and down, barefoot on the rocky ground, crying. A boy not much bigger than she vigorously pounded a prairie rattlesnake with an old shovel. Why were these children out here all alone?

A motherly desire to comfort them swelled in Anna's chest, and she rushed past Brett, keeping far away from the snake. She took the little girl in her arms. The child couldn't be much more than five.

"Shh. . .you're all right now." Trying to ignore the foul odor emanating from the child, Anna rubbed the girl's back, even though she remained stiff in her arms.

"Get back, boy."

Both children startled and looked up at Brett's command. The boy stepped back a half dozen feet. Brett walked over to the snake and nudged it with his rifle stock. "You killed it. That snake can't hurt you now, as long as you don't handle the head. You didn't get bit, did you?"

With the danger gone, the boy ignored Brett's question and spun toward Anna. "You let her go."

Brett laid his hand on the boy's shoulder, but the child shrugged it off. The girl wriggled and kicked her feet, so Anna set her on the ground. She limped over to the boy, who looked about seven or eight years old.

"Where you kids from?" Brett squatted to eye level with the children.

"It don't matter." The boy shrugged one thin shoulder. "C'mon, Emma."

Anna's heart nearly broke for the two urchins. Their clothes were little more than rags, and both were barefoot. Even with well-made shoes, Anna often found the rocky soil awkward to walk on. But barefoot? Why, their feet must be tattered.

"We have a buggy and can give you a ride," Anna offered.

"Please, Jimmy. I hurt my foot jumping on those rocks." Emma's soft blue eyes glistened.

The boy looked at her and Brett. "I don't see no buggy."

"It's just around the bend. I can carry you, Emma, if you need me to." Brett's warm smile must have softened the child's defenses, because she reached out her arms. Jimmy scowled when Brett picked up the girl, but he followed, grabbing his shovel as he passed the battered snake.

"We don't want to go back. Me and Emma are huntin' for our pa."

Brett exchanged a glance with Anna. These youngsters wouldn't survive out here alone. "It's best we take you back to wherever you came from. There are wild animals and all kinds of creatures in these hills that could hurt you, especially once the sun sets." Emma tightened her grip on Brett's neck.

"Besides"—Anna smiled sweetly to him—"people could be out looking for you. If night falls and you aren't home, people might risk their lives trying to find you."

Jimmy huffed a sarcastic laugh. "Ain't nobody lookin' for us, lady. I didn't figure my plan would work anyhow." Jimmy stared at the ground and kicked at a small rock. "Mr. Stout won't like you takin' us back. It's best we go alone."

Anna glanced at the boy. "Who is he?"

Jimmy shrugged. "The boss at the orphanage."

Anna blinked. She'd heard mumblings at church meetings just before visiting her mother in Bismarck that a couple had opened a children's home in the hills outside of Medora. After her frightening experience with the bank robbery, the orphanage had completely slipped her mind.

Brett loaded them in the crowded buggy and turned the horse up the trail. Anna didn't want to be rude, but the powerful stench of the children forced her to turn her head away. What kind of person could let such young children wander around alone and in such a horrid condition? She pressed her lips together, thinking she already didn't care for this Mr. Stout.

They traveled up the road Anna had wondered about earlier, and fifteen minutes later, they pulled up in front of an old clapboard house. The white paint had long ago lost its fight for survival with the elements. Two little girls, maybe three years old, in the same physical condition as Jimmy and Emma, rocked back and forth together in one rocker.

A man finely dressed in a white shirt, black pants, and a sateen vest shoved his way through the door and stared at them. His guarded gaze shifted to a friendly smile that Anna felt sure was forced. He reminded her of a traveling snake-oil salesman she'd once seen in town. "I see you've brought our runaways back. I'm deeply indebted to you folks."

Brett stopped the wagon and stepped down. Emma leaned against Anna as if she were afraid. Irritation fueled a fire growing within her. This man's clothing was new and of a high quality. His hair was oiled down, and his face cleanly shaven. She would bet he didn't smell like the children. How could he tend so well to his own ablutions and yet be oblivious to the children's needs? She wrapped her arm around Emma, wishing she could take the girl home. *Lord, protect these little ones.*

"Jimmy, Emma, hop on down. Miss Stout needs your help in the kitchen. We'll talk about your running away later." The man glared at the boy; then his gaze softened as he looked at Anna.

Emma cast a final glance at Anna before following Jimmy into the shabby house. She feared for the children and hoped they wouldn't be punished.

"Thank you for returning our kids. Jimmy seems determined to leave here and find his and Emma's father—the one who abandoned them when they were small." The man shook his head, a pitying expression on his face that Anna found difficult to believe.

"Forgive me for not introducing myself. I'm Lloyd Stout. My sister Hattie and I run this place. If not for us, these poor waifs would have nowhere to go. Most would probably be dead."

Brett touched the end of his hat but didn't offer Mr. Stout his hand. "Brett Wickham. And this is. . .Anna McFarland."

Anna's brow crinkled. Why had Brett stumbled over her name?

"My pleasure, Miss McFarland. It is Miss, isn't it?"

Anna nodded, uncomfortable with his unwavering appraisal. Brett watched the man silently with narrowed eyes. Did he, too, feel something was wrong?

"I do apologize for the condition things are in here. Donations to the facility have been lacking lately, even though we have more children than ever before."

Anna wanted to shout at him to spend less on himself and more on the children, but she doubted it would make a difference. One thing was certain: Even though Mr. Stout was rather nice looking, he would not be going on her list of potential suitors. She couldn't pin down what bothered her, but something wasn't right here.

"We need to get back on the road so we can make it home before dark." Brett climbed back into the buggy without even a good-bye. He made a smooching sound to the horse and jiggled the reins.

As the buggy jostled its way home, Anna realized she'd just found something worthwhile to invest her time and money in. She could make life better for those poor orphans.

nine

"You are not going back to that place alone." Quinn leaned toward her as if to emphasize his point.

"But I've been riding on this ranch alone as long as we've lived here." Anna figured it was futile to argue with her stubborn brother, but she had to try.

"That's different."

Anna pressed her hands to her hips. She could be stubborn, too. "How?"

Quinn blinked and straightened. "I don't have time to argue with you. If you insist on going to that orphanage, you'll take one of the hands with you."

Not Brett. She didn't like the confusing thoughts she had in his presence. It might be all right if he showed even the slightest interest in her, but most times, he was indifferent, even cold. On a rare occasion, though, she thought she had caught a glimpse of admiration in his sapphire gaze. Was he fighting an attraction to her, knowing her brother would never let one of their hands court her? Or maybe he had someone back home that he'd already given his heart to?

Quinn rubbed the back of his neck. "I've already assigned jobs to the men for today. Brett is the only one I can spare since he's not totally fit yet. But I'm still not convinced he's on the up-and-up. Take your rifle with you."

Anna sighed, resigning herself to another day with quiet Brett. "He's never been anything less than a gentleman, and he did protect me at risk to himself."

"I know, and that's the only reason I've let him drive you to town. I reckon if he was willing to risk his life for you when he didn't even know you, that you're safe with him now." Her brother slapped on his hat. "I'll have him hitch the buggy."

"I really need to exercise Bella. Do you think Brett's healed enough to ride that far?"

Quinn nodded. "He's been riding some of the green broke horses and doing fine."

He strode out the front door. Anna headed into the kitchen to get the fresh loaves of cinnamon bread that Leyna had made for the children. The scent of sweet baked goods had permeated the house all morning.

"I wrapped the bread in paper and put it in here." Leyna held up the burlap bag. "You will tie it onto your saddle, ja?"

Anna smiled. "That should work perfectly. The children will love your treat. Thank you for making it for them." She hugged the cook; then Leyna handed her a smaller flour sack.

"I packed lunch for you and *Herr* Brett."

Anna lifted her brows at Leyna's humorous smirk. "How did you know Brett would be going with me today?"

Leyna shrugged. "I just pray, is all."

"Don't bother trying to matchmake us. He has shown no interest in me."

Leyna tsk-tsked and stirred a bowl of batter. "Young people, what do they know? I see how *Herr* Brett watches you."

Brett watches me?

A warm sensation started in the pit of her stomach and crept through her body, warming her down to her toes. Was it possible he liked her but was afraid to show it?

Anna took the bags from Leyna and moseyed outside. The day suddenly gleamed brighter, and she now looked forward to the ride to town and back with eagerness.

&

The last thing Brett wanted to do today was escort Lottie to town. The men in the bunkhouse were already teasing that she was sweet on him. The problem was, he liked this side of the female outlaw. The compassion she had for those smelly orphans just about undid him. He had to keep a barrier up where she was concerned. He couldn't allow her soft side to sway him when he of all people knew what she and her brother were capable of. *Those Sallingers are such great actors; they ought to be in the theater.*

Brett shook his head as he led Jasper and Bella out of the barn. Anna's brother had said he'd be escorting her back to the orphanage. He wouldn't mind another look at that dilapidated place. Something fishy was going on there, and he was glad for a chance to figure out what it was. Those poor kids looked mistreated and half starved, while the man who ran the children's home was well fed and immaculately dressed—so much so that he didn't fit there.

The lawman in him simmered. He had no patience for people who mistreated children.

"What's got you in such a dither?"

Brett stopped in front of Lottie, blinking. "What?"

"I said good morning and you never even heard me—and you're scowling."

She looked beautiful in that baby blue shirt and brown riding skirt. Her straw hat hung on her back, its thin cord cutting along her soft throat, making a slight indentation. She carried a large burlap sack and a smaller bag, both bulging.

Brett swallowed and took the sacks from her, tying the smaller one onto Bella's saddle and the larger one to Jasper's. He shouldn't be wondering how soft Lottie's skin was. She pulled her hat onto her sun-kissed hair. He looped Bella's reins over her neck and locked his hands together to boost Lottie up. She quirked a brow at him but allowed him to assist her. In spite of being over five and a half feet tall, she was light as a cloud. Brett shook his head, reminding himself to never do undercover work again. He needed to keep his distance to keep his perspective from getting skewed. His father's harsh words still haunted him. *"You're too softhearted to be a lawman, Brett."*

Lord, help me. Give me wisdom to see justice done and not be swayed by Lottie's beautiful smile or soft touch.

Things seemed overly quiet as they rode up to the orphanage. On the trip there, Lottie had expressed her concern for the children. So she'd noticed, too.

On second look, the house was in worse condition than Brett remembered. Nearly all the paint had worn off, leaving a tired, weathered two-story structure that leaned a smidgen to the right. Any grass near the house had been trampled long ago, leaving only dirt and rocks now. There were no children to be seen.

Lottie cast him a worried glance. "You don't suppose they cleared out, do you?"

The thought had crossed his mind, but he doubted Lloyd Stout would have gone to such trouble. And why should he? It's not as if the man cared about the children that much.

Lottie tied Bella to the porch, removed the large burlap sack from Brett's saddle, and knocked on the door. After a second knock, two tiny urchins came running to the open door, looking uncertain whether to invite them inside. The sun hadn't even crested to noon, and yet these toddlers were filthy. Their clothes were frayed rags, and their hair hung limp and tangled. Did they ever get a bath? Brett's heart twisted for the poor little kids.

A tall, thin woman with sharp features appeared behind the children. "May I help you?"

"We were here yesterday. Met a Mr. Stout. We're the ones who found Jimmy and Emma and returned them." Lottie shifted the bag on her shoulder.

Brett dismounted and ground-tied Jasper, keeping his eye on the children. Both of them leaned against the door frame instead of hiding behind the woman's skirts like most shy youngsters would do. Interesting.

The woman's features softened a bit. "Oh, yes, my brother told me about you. I'm Hattie Stout."

Brett resisted chuckling. Stout might describe Hattie's brother, but she was the opposite.

Lottie held up the burlap sack. "We brought you some cinnamon bread and some other things. I also want to offer my services. Is there anything I can help you with?"

The woman's surprised gray eyes sparked a second before dulling again. "Thank you, but I don't think my brother would like me accepting help. He thinks I should be able to handle things here."

"Where are the other children?"

Brett wondered where Lloyd Stout was, too, but didn't ask.

Miss Stout's expression looked panicked for a split second.

Lottie glanced over her shoulder at him. "Why. . .they're at school, of course."

School. *Sure.* If he were a betting man, he'd be willing to bet they weren't at school by the woman's reaction to Lottie's question. But where else could they be?

He stepped onto the porch, and Miss Stout stepped back—a typical response for a woman afraid of men. Her gaze darted from him to Lottie. Up close, he could see that one of the children had a runny nose. He reached down to pat the waif, but she dodged his hand and ran back into the house.

"They don't take too kindly to strangers, you know. They're afraid someone will take them away from us."

Uh-huh. If he believed that, he'd be a sucker for every peddler in the country. More likely they'd been punished for talking to strangers.

"It must be difficult caring for so many children. Why don't you let me bathe these two little ones while you do whatever you were doing before we arrived?"

Miss Stout looked down at the floor. "I guess it wouldn't hurt none if you washed them young'uns, just so long as you're gone before my brother returns."

"Wonderful!" Lottie's sweet smile made Brett wish she wasn't an outlaw. Made him wish for things that could never be.

She turned to face him. "I don't suppose you could work on some things outside the house? Maybe fix the steps?"

Brett glanced at Miss Stout. "You got a hammer and nails? Some spare wood?"

She blinked, then shook her head.

"You could get some at the mercantile. Just put them on our account," Lottie said. "I'll probably be awhile, getting those babies clean, so you'd have plenty of time if you want to go now."

"Will you be all right?" Brett's train of thought shocked him.

Lottie reached out and touched his arm, sending hot and cold chills charging upward as if he'd been hit by lightning. He wanted to step back and yet step forward at the same time, but he held his ground. "Thank you for your concern, but I'll be fine. See you in a bit."

The dilapidated house swallowed her into its dark mouth. Brett swung away, irritated with himself for worrying about an outlaw's well-being. He leaped onto Jasper. What had gotten into him?

Ten minutes later, he rode into Medora. A letter to Marshal Cronan burned his pocket, and he was thankful for the chance to get away from Lottie for a while. He'd wanted to send a telegraph but had chosen the more private letter to update his superior on where he was and what he was doing. The marshal should be pleased to learn he'd infiltrated the Sallingers' hideout so easily. Brett rubbed his chest where the healing scars itched. Well. . .maybe not so easily.

He paid the postage for the letter and collected the supplies he needed to do some minor repairs at the children's home. After tying them to his saddle, he looked around town for someone who might be willing to give him some information. He found just the man sitting on a bench outside the saloon.

"Buy a feller who's down on his luck a drink, Mister?" The bewhiskered old man glanced up with red-rimmed, amber-colored eyes.

Brett stopped and rubbed his chin. Whiskey had a way of loosening a man's lips, but as a Christian, buying liquor didn't sit well with him. "How about I treat you to a hot lunch at the café? I don't particularly like to eat alone."

The man licked his lips and glanced at the saloon door. "I guess I could eat something, if yer willin' to pay for it. The name's Ollie."

The café taunted Brett with its fragrant scents. He sat at a table in the back with Ollie, and both ordered the fried chicken. The soft hum of conversation blended with the clinking of silverware.

"So, what do you want to know?"

Brett peered at Ollie and grinned. The old-timer was sharper than he looked. "What do you know about that orphanage outside of town?"

Ollie shrugged, and his suspender slipped off his frail shoulder. The man would need warmer clothes before winter set in. "Not much. I hear that kids come and go quite a lot. Seems they tend to get lost too often. Don't care much for the snake that runs the place. I'm betting he takes all the donation money for hisself."

"Where do the kids come from?"

"Don't know. Orphan train, maybe?"

That didn't make sense to Brett. The orphan trains tried to find good homes for children, rather than moving them from an Eastern orphanage to another one out West. Brett searched the chambers of his memory. Hadn't he seen a notice about a missing child back in Marshal Cronan's office? Could the two things be related? "Ever heard of kids gone missing in these parts?"

Ollie's eyes rolled up, as if he were searching his mind for an answer. "Nah. Most folks in these parts look after their own. They may be from somewheres else though."

"Know anything about the McFarlands?"

The old man grinned, his yellow teeth as crooked as a New York politician. "Yep, that I do know about. Their old man rode into town one day and paid cash for the Stonecreek Ranch. Then he bought several smaller ranches bordering Stonecreek and changed the name to the Rocking M."

The same woman Brett had seen at the café before set their plates in front of them. Ollie grabbed his fork and dug in. Brett let the conversation subside while they ate. When his food was gone, Ollie sopped up the leftover gravy from his potatoes with his roll.

"Mmm, mmm. That sure tasted good. I thank ya kindly."

Brett nodded once. "You're welcome. I've heard a few folks around here don't like the McFarlands. Why's that?"

Ollie pushed his plate back. "Guess it's because some folks didn't like how old man McFarland bought out their friends' ranches after we had some terrible winters. Then, too, them McFarlands shop mostly in Bismarck, and the store owners here don't like that."

"That seems like a petty reason to me."

Ollie shrugged and slid his suspender back over his shoulder. "Small town loyalties, ya know. Now me, I'm gonna find that big gold shipment that was lost in the Badlands. Then I'll make ever'body happy 'cause I'll shop all the stores in town." He grinned and leaned back in his chair.

Brett remembered the payroll shipment that had been stolen from a Northern Pacific train several years back. The robbers had been captured, but the gold was never found. Rumor was they'd buried it somewhere in the Badlands. Brett had searched these hills with several other marshals but never found the lost gold. It figured there would still be stories circulating.

Most likely, the Sallingers had taken the money and used it to expand their ranch. Brett tossed some coins on the table and stood. "Nice chatting with you, Ollie."

The old man nodded. "Guess I'll just sit here while I drink some more coffee." He smiled and lifted his cup.

Brett nodded and walked out of the café, worrying about Lottie. Was she safe at the orphanage? What would Lloyd Stout do if he returned and found her there?

He glanced at the sun's position in the sky. He'd been gone much longer than he should have been. Settling the planks of wood for the steps across his lap, he nudged Jasper back toward the children's home, his thoughts and emotions swirling.

ten

"You wouldn't believe the condition of that place, Quinn." Anna sliced off a circle of bratwurst and stuck it in her mouth, along with some of Leyna's sauerkraut. Guilt riddled her as the tangy, salty flavor teased her taste buds. Here she was eating a delicious meal when the orphans were eating who knows what. She had to win Quinn over to helping them. "Those poor children are filthy. They don't have decent clothes or shoes, and they look as if they haven't eaten a good meal in months. My heart nearly broke."

Quinn's mouth pinched into a straight line. "I can't abide people abusing children, but I don't know what we can do about it. Maybe talk to the sheriff."

Anna laid her fork down. "Leyna and I were talking. What if we started a foundation to help the children?"

"What's the point of that? Sounds to me like that Stout man would just spend any money donated on himself." Quinn scooped three heaping spoons of applesauce onto his plate then proceeded to shovel it into his mouth.

"We find good people to run that place and kick out those bad ones." Leyna refilled Quinn's cup with coffee, not the least bit sorry for interrupting their conversation.

"Good idea. But who is actually in charge of the orphanage? Who do we talk to about getting changes made?"

"I'll see if I can find out. Maybe one Saturday we could take a crew to town and have a workday." Quinn sat with his elbows on the table, sipping his coffee. "I don't know about this foundation thing, though. Much of our money is tied up in the ranch."

Ideas swirled through Anna's mind. "Maybe Grandma could get her church involved. The old ladies there like to sew for the unfortunates. Mother would be happy to help with it, I'm sure."

Her brother nodded. "That's not a half-bad idea."

Anna smiled, grateful that he agreed with her. "I'll need to get a list of all the children and what size clothing they wear. But I don't know how agreeable the Stouts will be." She frowned at her brother. "Miss Stout didn't even want to let me in the house. Once I got in, I could see why. It's not much of a place. Though the rooms were fairly clean, the old furniture was threadbare, what there was of it."

"I imagine furniture wouldn't hold up too well in a house with—what'd you say?—a dozen or so kids."

"I don't really know how many children there are. The older ones haven't been around when we've been there." Anna spun some kraut onto her fork. "And I don't think their furniture is ragged because of the little ones. It looks as if it was someone else's rejects."

"Might have been. Probably most all the furnishings in the home were donated, and folks generally don't get rid of furniture until it's past worn out." He stabbed a hunk of bratwurst.

Anna's gaze drifted to the parlor. They'd brought their furniture with them from Texas when they moved here. The horsehair couch was old but had many years of life left in it. She'd never considered redecorating the parlor before because it was still serviceable. But now. . .

Filled with an eagerness she couldn't contain, she turned her gaze back to her brother. "What if—"

"No."

"But—"

"No!"

Anna leaned back in her chair and crossed her arms. "You

don't even know what I was going to say."

Quinn grinned. "I saw you eyeing our furniture with the look of a trout after a fat, ol' worm."

"Well. . .so what? It's old."

"It's fine."

"You're so stubborn." She tossed her head and looked out the window.

"That's the pot calling the kettle black." Quinn chuckled as he stood. "We'll find some way to help. Let me think on it—and don't go hauling away our furniture."

She watched him snatch his hat off the peg and leave. She speared another slice of meat and chewed it as if chomping up her frustrating brother. At least he agreed to find some way to help. That was something she could be thankful for.

"You could maybe get some of the townswomen to help out?" Leyna removed the bowl of kraut and Quinn's plate.

"Why do you suppose they aren't already helping out?"

"Could be they are."

"I've never organized anything before, but I can talk to some of the church women and see if they'd like to help." Anna shrugged. "But even if they did, I don't know if the Stouts would accept our help. Hattie seemed quite offended that I offered to wash those two toddlers."

"We will just have to pray about it. God will show us what we can do to help."

Anna nodded. She would pray, but her mind raced with all manner of ideas now that she had finally found something worthwhile in which to invest her time.

❧

The buckboard creaked and groaned over the rocky trail, knocking Anna's shoulder into Brett's. She glanced out the corner of her eye at the handsome man. He'd been quiet ever since leaving the ranch. She supposed he was getting tired of escorting her to town.

If she allowed her imagination to take flight, she could pretend they were married. Mrs. Brett Wickham sounded lovely.

She heaved a sigh at her schoolgirl silliness. At twenty-two, she was closer to being a spinster.

Brett mumbled something, drawing her attention. The sun had browned his skin. His blue eyes and white teeth only enhanced his dark coloring. A scowl tugged at his features.

"Is something wrong?"

Brett rubbed the back of his neck and slid a glance her way. He went back to studying the trail ahead. "It doesn't matter."

"What doesn't?" Now he had her curiosity aroused.

He lifted his hat and ran his hands through his hair, the same color as the chocolate fudge she'd sampled in a Bismarck candy store.

"I probably shouldn't tell you, but you'll hound me all day if I don't. Some of the guys are teasing me about being your nursemaid and not doing any real work."

Anna crossed her arms and leaned back against the hard seat. The men at the ranch all liked her, so why would they tease about such a thing? She looked across the grasslands at the hills on the horizon.

"Look, this isn't about you." Brett turned toward her on the seat. "It's just that I can't get anything done at the ranch when I'm escorting you all the time."

"Well, I never asked you to." No, but she'd asked Quinn if Brett could escort her. She forced a scowl, sure that it bettered the one he'd worn earlier. "I've been riding this country alone for nearly a third of my life. I'm not a baby and don't need anyone tending me." She leaned in closer. "In fact, just turn this wagon around and go back home."

≈

Brett heaved a sigh, smelling of coffee. "I knew I shouldn't have mentioned it. And besides, look what happened last week with the bear."

"Well. . .well. . .that was an isolated incident."

This time he leaned in. "But you nearly got yourself killed. I'm here to see that doesn't happen again."

Up this close, his blue eyes had almost a navy ring around them. His breath wafted over her face. If she leaned a little closer, she could kiss him. And she knew that she wanted to taste him on her lips. Would he mind?

She looked at his eyes again and saw that he was watching *her* lips. Anna's breath caught in her throat. The wagon dipped, knocking their foreheads together in a painful clunk.

How embarrassing! She faced forward and refused to look at Brett. Had he been about to kiss her? Disappointment battled with relief. What was she thinking?

Looking out across the landscape, she scoured the area, hoping nobody had seen them. Quinn would never let a ranch hand court her, not even one who'd saved her life. She needed to curb her infatuation with Brett, because there was no future for them together.

Having him as her escort didn't help matters. Maybe she should ask Quinn to let Claude drive her. But time sure would pass much slower than it did with Brett, even if he didn't talk all that much.

As they pulled up in front of the children's home an hour later, the two toddlers she'd washed the day before sat in the front porch rocker. Their sunken eyes widened at the sight of her and Brett. The dark-haired waif on the right lifted one hand and waved, but the blond looked frightened.

Brett stopped the buckboard in front of the door and climbed down. He lifted his hands to assist Anna, but she was tempted to climb down the other side alone. Realizing the pettiness of her thoughts, she placed her hands on Brett's shoulders. He lifted her at the waist and set her on the ground. Her hands ran down his arms in a daring gesture as he stared at her with that look of his that made her tremble. Was he thinking about their almost kiss?

Brett stepped away and hoisted a twenty-five-pound sack of flour onto his shoulder. His free hand rubbed across his chest, fingers splayed.

"You shouldn't be lifting such heavy things until your stitches have been removed. Did you hurt yourself?"

"I'm fine." He strode toward the door, his scowl planted back on his handsome face.

The toddlers scrambled off the chair and darted through the open door. Anna knocked on the door frame. Miss Stout soon answered, a damp dishcloth drying her hands.

"Oh, it's you again. What do you want now?" She eyed the bag on Brett's shoulder.

"May we come in and talk to you?" Anna asked. "I have some ideas for helping you and your brother with the children, and we've brought you some supplies."

"Lloyd don't want you two coming around no more. I got in trouble for letting you in yesterday."

"Could Mr. Wickham at least put this sack of flour in your kitchen? He's had a recent injury and shouldn't even be lifting it."

Miss Stout's gaze flitted back and forth between them. "I didn't order no flour."

"It's a gift from the Rocking M Ranch. We've got some sugar, bread, and a few other things in the wagon, too."

The woman's eyes brightened at the mention of sugar, and she stepped back. "The kitchen's this way. I sure hope I don't get hollered at for this. At least I can make Lloyd a cake now. He does like his sweets."

Anna pursed her lips. "The donations are for the children, not particularly Mr. Stout."

"Well, I know that. I didn't mean nothin' by it."

Brett set the bag on the floor of the big kitchen. An old

cast-iron stove took up one corner with a worktable beside it. A basin of water and a stack of clean dishes and mismatched cups cluttered the counter. On the far wall was a large, worn table with two chairs at each end and benches on the sides. No paint, wallpaper, or pictures adorned the plain wood walls. The back door stood open like the front, and one lone window near the stove was open. A cool but comfortable breeze blew through the room.

"I'll fetch the other bags." Brett rolled his shoulders as he left the room.

Anna's gaze followed him. She turned her focus back on Miss Stout.

"I want to help you improve things here for the children. I thought I could measure each child to see what size they wear and then get my grandmother's sewing circle to make each child a set of clothes."

Miss Stout fiddled with the edge of her frayed apron. "Lloyd ain't gonna like that. He thinks we's the only ones what should take care of them young'uns."

Anna wanted to win this woman to her side for the sake of the children. "I understand, but you have what—a dozen children?"

"Eleven."

"Surely any woman with eleven children would need help. What's the age of the oldest?"

"I don't know for sure. Maybe twelve."

The two urchins from the porch peered around the doorjamb when Brett carried in the bag of sugar. He dumped it beside the flour and left again, the children scattering as he walked in their direction.

"How many little ones are here? I've seen two. Are there more?"

"Just one. He's asleep."

"How old are they?" Anna walked back into the parlor,

looking for the little ones. She stepped back as Brett carried in a crate of various canned fruits and vegetables.

"Don't really know. Two. Three maybe."

Anna spun around, making Miss Stout's eyes go wide. "How can you not know their ages? Where do the children come from?"

Miss Stout retreated back to the worktable. She picked up a mug and dried it, then set it aside and picked up another. "Lloyd generally finds the young'uns. Once in a while someone will bring us one. Nobody never tells me their age."

Hattie was getting defensive, so Anna dropped the age topic. "Do you mind if I measure the younger children for clothes?"

Miss Stout shrugged. "Guess it wouldn't hurt none. Junie, Suzanne, you two get in here."

The woman finished drying another cup and watched the doorway. When the children didn't come, she smacked the tin mug down hard on the counter. "Don't make me get my switch. You two get in here."

The patter of tiny bare feet announced the arrival of the two waifs as they ran into the room. Both looked frightened half to death.

Anna's heart melted. The poor dears. She knelt down and looked them in the eye. "Remember me from yesterday? We had fun when I gave you both a bath."

Junie nodded, but Suzanne only sucked her thumb and clung to Junie's shabby dress.

"Well. . .I know some nice ladies who want to make you some new clothes, and I need to measure you so they know how big to make them. Is that all right?"

Junie nodded again. Anna made quick order of measuring the two and then the baby boy who slept in a dresser drawer on a dingy blanket. Anna wanted to be angry with the Stouts, but the fact of the matter was, they *had* given the children a home when nobody else wanted them. Granted it wasn't much, but they had a roof over them and food to eat. She tried not to judge the Stouts too severely for not doing a better job. Raising eleven children was a huge job, especially if you weren't related to them.

"Thank you, Miss Stout. I'll be able to send these measurements on ahead of the others so the women can get started on them." She hadn't exactly asked the sewing group yet, but she knew their hearts, having visited her grandmother and met her friends.

"Everything's unloaded. Are you done?" Brett stood in the doorway, filling up the whole opening.

"I suppose." Junie and Suzanne could already use another bath, but they'd probably go hide if they knew her thoughts.

Brett handed Anna up into the wagon and joined her. As the buckboard pulled away from the house, Anna looked over her shoulder. Junie and Suzanne were climbing back into their rocker.

Now that she thought about it, she hadn't seen a single toy. Maybe she could make some dolls for the girls—if she'd ever learn to sew. "I need to go into town before we head home."

Brett peered at her with raised brows but guided the wagon toward Medora at the fork instead of the Rocking M.

As they passed the tiny schoolhouse a few minutes later, Anna got an idea. "Stop! Stop!"

Brett yanked back on the reins and spun toward her. "What's wrong?" His gaze took her in then checked out the area around them as he reached for his rifle.

Anna giggled. "Sorry. I didn't mean to alarm you. I just thought since we were at the schoolhouse that I could see if it would be possible to measure the other children. It would speed things up tremendously, because I want to mail a letter with their sizes to my grandma while we're in town."

Brett's sighs were getting familiar. He shook his head and

helped her down. About a dozen children played in the yard, but she didn't see Jimmy and Emma. Brett followed her, dodging the lunch pails and containers lining the stairs. Inside, a young woman sat behind a desk. The room smelled of wood and chalk dust.

"May I help you?"

Anna introduced herself and Brett. "I'm helping gather clothing for the children at the orphanage. I was wondering if you'd mind my measuring the orphans while I'm here."

The pretty blond scrunched up her nose. "I don't see what that has to do with me."

Anna moved closer. "I just thought since you're the teacher I should ask your permission before approaching them."

The teacher stood. "I think there's been some kind of mistake. None of the children from the orphanage attend school here. I was under the impression they were taught at the home."

eleven

Lottie sidled a worried glance at Brett. "Uh. . .we were led to believe the older children were at school."

The teacher wrung her hands. "Oh, dear. This is highly irregular. I'll have to talk to Mr. Richter, the school board chairman. Although I don't know how I'd handle any more children than I have now."

"Don't worry about it, ma'am. We'll find out what's going on. I'm sure we just misunderstood." Brett took hold of Lottie's arm and ushered her out the door. In spite of her bewildered look, she didn't fight him.

"Why did you say we misunderstood?"

As they descended the steps, Brett glanced over his shoulder to make sure the door had closed. "I'm not ready for that teacher to stir things up and alert Stout that we're suspicious of him."

She leaned against his side as they headed for the buggy, causing a stirring within that he didn't want to acknowledge. "I knew something wasn't right over there. What do you think's going on?"

"I don't know, but I aim to find out." He helped her into the wagon, climbed in, then guided it on into town and stopped at the sheriff's office. They stepped inside, but the office was empty.

Lottie casually studied a wooden door with a small barred window that Brett assumed led to the jail cells. "Now what?"

"I don't know." He tried to rub the tension out of the back of his neck, halfway surprised that Lottie hadn't bucked at the idea of entering the sheriff's office. She'd just marched right in as if she'd never once done anything illegal. Even now she seemed completely at ease. "Unless. . ."

"Unless what?"

He stared out the window for a moment, hoping to see the sheriff. He had some questions for the man. "I could come back in the morning and trail the older kids. See where Stout takes them."

"I'll ride with you."

"No." He spun to face her. "It could be dangerous."

"I'm not afraid. I've been in dangerous situations before."

Brett clenched his jaw. He just bet she had. He stared into her coffee-colored eyes, wishing things were different. What was he looking for? Guilt?

Her cheeks flushed a bright pink at his perusal, and she looked away. "Fine."

Lord, why does the only woman I ever wanted have to be an outlaw?

If only. . .

He stormed out the door toward the post office with Lottie on his heels. *"You're too soft. . ."* His father's words haunted him again. Maybe he was right.

All Brett needed was some evidence tying Jack and Lottie to the bank robbery; then he could go home and start a new chapter in his life. He had to get inside the McFarland house again.

His boots echoed on the wooden floor as he strode into the post office. "Got any letters for Brett Wickham?" he asked the postmaster.

The thin man shook his head. "No, haven't received nothing for you. Sorry."

Brett nodded his thanks. Lottie sashayed past him to the counter.

"I'd like to purchase two sheets of paper and an envelope with postage to Bismarck." She turned to Brett. "Do you mind waiting while I pen a note to my grandmother?"

He shook his head and went outside. Leaning against a post, he thought about Lloyd Stout. What could he be doing with the older children?

Lottie had told him that Hattie had said her brother was the one who usually brought the children to the orphanage. So. . .where was he finding them?

Brett marched back inside. Lottie peeked up from her letter writing and smiled. His insides turned to liquid fire, knowing that smile was for him alone. He was in big trouble.

Focusing back on the task at hand, he stopped at the counter. "Could you answer a question for me?"

"I'll try." The postmaster stacked a pile of envelopes he was sorting.

"Did you ever hear of any children going missing in these parts?"

The man narrowed his gaze. "That's an odd question."

"Humor me."

"Well, not so much around here, but there *have* been some stories over the past years of children around Dickinson and even as far off as Mandan and Bismarck going missing."

"Hmm. . ." With the train, a trip to Bismarck could be done in half a day or less. Stout could easily travel to another town, find a child, and bring it back to the orphanage with nobody the wiser, leaving a set of grieving parents behind to wonder what happened to their beloved child. The lawman in him smelled a rat. Still, he had no proof.

Lottie sealed her envelope and handed it to the postmaster. Brett followed her outside into the sunny afternoon, trying hard to ignore how the sun glistened on the golden hair that hung below her straw hat. Swallowing hard, he thought of what he'd do with Lloyd Stout if his suspicions were right. The problem was, he no longer had a badge, and he'd risk Lottie finding out he was a lawman if he made a move on the Stouts.

A man dressed in a stiff white shirt and black pants jogged toward Lottie. "I thought I saw you in town, Miss McFarland. Got a telegram for you."

Lottie paid the man and opened the thin paper. She gasped and looked up at Brett. "My mother is coming home on Friday. That's such a surprise since she told me she planned to stay in Bismarck. I wonder what changed her mind."

Brett knew she must be happy since her mother had been gone so long.

"Oh, dear. We have so much to do. We need to air out her room, and. . ." Her cheeks flushed. "You aren't interested in all that."

She snagged his arm and tugged him down the street. "I need to stop at the mercantile and get some more fabric. I want to make dolls for those little girls. Did you notice they didn't have any toys at all?"

Brett shook his head. He hadn't thought of such a trivial detail, although now that he did, he wondered about it. Why wouldn't an orphanage have some toys? Maybe they were in a playroom instead of the parlor, not that the place looked big enough to have a separate play area.

Excitement glittered in Lottie's eyes. "I'm not a very good seamstress, but I hope it's not too late to learn. I just never cared about sewing for myself, but I think making something for the orphans would be very satisfying."

Suddenly, she stopped and spun toward him. "Oh! I should telegraph Ma and have her bring more supplies to replenish the ones we gave the children's home."

Just that fast, she was off in another direction, tugging him along as if he belonged to her and had nothing else to do but her bidding. He shook his head, frustrated that he didn't mind at all. Glancing heavenward, he cast another plea to God. So far his prayers to distance his heart weren't working. If he didn't find evidence soon, he just might have to leave and allow another lawman to do that task. He didn't like failing, but he could not allow himself to fall in love with an outlaw—and he feared that was close to happening.

He halted in his tracks, jerking Lottie to a stop. She looked at him. "What's wrong?"

"You go tend to your errands. I. . .uh. . .have some things I need to do."

Her warm smile added salt to his wounded heart. "All right. I'll meet you at the wagon in a half hour or so."

Spinning around, Brett strode away. Out of politeness, he nodded to a couple he passed as he crossed the street. Lottie had confessed her hatred for sewing before, so why was she willing to do something she disliked so that she could make some dolls for the children? How could a cold-blooded outlaw care so much about a handful of dirty kids?

Oh, he cared, too, but then he wasn't a man on the run. Could it be Jack had forced Lottie to take part in the robberies? If she'd never killed anyone and was willing to testify against her brother, she might be able to get a lighter sentence.

But she'd benefited greatly from the money stolen in the robberies. She had one of the nicest homes he'd seen in the whole area, and a fine ranch that seemed to be successful.

At the buckboard, Brett unhitched the horses and led them to a trough. After they drank their fill, he found a patch of grass and hobbled the animals so they could graze for a short while.

Leaning against a tree, he watched a hawk gliding high in the sky. Lazy, feathery clouds drifted by as the warm sun burned the last of the morning's chill away. He thought of Taylor. His brother had been so excited to see him again and to share the news of his successful cattle drive. Taylor had a promising future. Some pretty gal would have snagged his attention—if she hadn't already. The fact that he didn't even know if his brother had been sweet on a gal nagged at him.

He should have known. Should have written more. Should have gone home more often.

But he hadn't, and his own stubbornness had cost him the last years he could have had with Taylor. Lottie captured his gaze as she walked toward him carrying a large package, her light green skirt swishing back and forth like a bell. She looked so young and deceptively innocent. She waved and smiled, making his pulse race. He sniffed a laugh. How ironic that his heart would deceive him—would play the outlaw in desiring a woman he could never have. Striding toward the horses, he struggled to keep the picture of his brother's limp body in his mind. Cold and dead.

No female thief was going to steal his heart. He refused to allow it.

⁂

Anna watched the North Dakota landscape slowly drift by as the wagon headed toward home. Brett's constant mood changes were more perplexing than trying to figure out the North Dakota weather. One moment he was smiling at her, the next he was scowling. Anna wasn't sure if he actually liked her or just tolerated her.

Oh, there were times she was sure he cared for her, like when he'd stare deeply into her eyes, and then there was the time she thought for sure he would kiss her. But he'd never voiced an interest in her and seemed to just be doing his job. Anna sighed. Why did men have to be so perplexing?

What would it be like to have a man like her enough to not kowtow to Quinn? Maybe more men would come calling after her mother returned. Before Ellen went to Bismarck, they'd even had Saturday visitors on occasion, but not for the past year. If only Grandma would move to the ranch, then her mother could stay permanently, but she wasn't ready to give up her home and friends.

Anna's shoulder bumped into Brett's arm as the wagon

dipped into another rut. Tingles shot through her body, and she rubbed her arm from shoulder to elbow. Why did his touch affect her so?

She shook her head, trying to dislodge the confusing thoughts of her escort, and considered how to go about making a doll. She'd gotten plain linen for the faces and various yardages of different colored fabric to make clothes with. There was also some extra heavy thread for the facial features, and even yellow and brown yarn for hair. Maybe they could make the dolls' hair and eye color match the children? That would work for the girls, but what about the boys?

A rabbit zigzagged across the road up ahead. She watched until it disappeared under a juniper shrub. Off to her right, the Badlands' buttes rose up in a majestic display. She often thought that God must have been angry when He created this part of the country. While the Badlands held a craggy beauty of its own, most folks considered this area rugged and barren. And yet amid all the rocks and boulders, God had created bountiful grasslands, perfect for raising cattle—if they could survive the tough winters.

Bored with the silence, she turned to Brett. "Do you think you'll ever go back to your ranch?"

He stared ahead, his expression blank. "Probably."

"You never told me if you have any siblings."

A muscle in his cheek quivered. "I had a younger brother, but he's dead."

Anna laid her hand on his arm, drawing his gaze. "I'm so sorry, Brett. Quinn can be bossy and stubborn, but I'm thankful I have him. I can't imagine what it would be like to lose him. It's hard enough not having Adam at home, even though I know that one day he and Mariah will return."

Brett scowled and refocused on the road. Obviously, he wasn't in a talking mood. Again. She liked him more than any man she'd ever met, and yet she knew so little about him. And it looked as if she wasn't going to learn any more today. At least she no longer thought he was a rustler. Rustlers wouldn't attend church or show such an interest in parentless children.

She allowed her thoughts to drift to the orphans. What could Mr. Stout be doing with the older ones? She had no idea but was determined to find out.

ð

Back home in her room, Anna stared in the mirror as she untied her straw hat. Did Brett find her pretty? She'd always wished she had blue eyes like Adam's. Even though he was her twin, she looked more like Quinn.

She needed a bath to get the layer of dust off her after the long trip to town and back. Next time she took the wagon, she'd take a book. When Brett wasn't in the mood to talk, the trip was quite boring. One could only look at rocks and grass for so long.

She pulled open a drawer and tugged out her nightgown. Her gaze landed on the glimmering gold coins from the bank. They'd skipped her mind. She really needed to return them. After her bath, she'd see if Quinn had forty dollars in paper money to replace the coins. Then she'd pen a letter to the bank explaining how the double-eagles had accidentally fallen into her reticule when that female outlaw knocked her down. Shivering at the memory, Anna laid the coins on her dresser and went to take a bath.

twelve

The morning sun crested over the rocky buttes east of the Rocking M. Anna pushed Bella hard, anxious to arrive at the orphanage before Lloyd Stout could leave with the older children. After being locked in a corral for days, her mare eagerly responded to Anna's gentle nudge to run faster.

The cool morning breeze whipped dust in Anna's face and made her eyes water, but it felt exhilarating to be on horseback again. She'd never ride in a buggy or wagon if she didn't have to.

A herd of mule deer dashed away when Bella cantered through a pass and startled them. The animals scattered in three directions, darting back and forth, joining up again before they disappeared over the next hill.

Anna peeked over her shoulder and smiled, knowing she'd managed to sneak away without Quinn or Brett finding out. She'd left Leyna a note that she'd gone riding and wouldn't be there for breakfast. The slice of bread and cheese she'd eaten would sustain her for now.

As she neared the orphanage, she slowed Bella to a walk and allowed the mare to cool down. She located a nice little draw, where Bella could graze and be fairly well hidden, and dismounted. After securing her mare, Anna climbed up to the top of the nearest butte and jogged forward until the roof of the orphanage came into view.

Ducking low, she hurried to a large red cedar tree guarding the valley below like a lone sentinel. A thin trail of smoke drifted up from the kitchen area of the orphanage. From her vantage point, Anna could see that the roof needed immediate attention, but if she were to tell Brett or Quinn that, they'd want to know how she knew. Better they find out for themselves.

Squatting behind the trunk of the cedar, she waited. Half an hour later, two older boys who looked almost in their teens came out the back door. One headed to the privy while the other began tugging tools out of a lean-to affixed to the back of the house and tossing them on the ground.

Soon, children of varying sizes came outside and searched through the pile of rusted shovels and picks until each found a specific one. Anna counted the children. Eight. With the three smaller ones left in Hattie's care, that made eleven. So the woman hadn't lied about that.

Lloyd Stout exited the house and stretched. The largest boy came out of a dilapidated barn leading a healthy buckskin. Mr. Stout took the reins, looped them over the horse's neck, and climbed on—not without some effort on his part. He yelled something to the children, but Anna couldn't make out the words.

Anger bolted through her as the ragtag group of barefoot children plodded after their leader, each carrying a tool. Why, Mr. Stout's horse looked better fed than those poor kids. She watched until the group went around a bend and she could no longer see them. She debated whether to follow on foot or horseback, and finally opted on riding Bella. At least the mare would be nearby if she needed a quick getaway.

Bella carefully made her way down a steep incline just past the orphanage, and Anna easily picked up the trail. Obviously, the children had walked this path many times, because there were multiple footprints both heading toward and away from the home.

Close to a mile past the orphanage, the children diverted to a smaller path that led between two buttes. On either side of her were a multitude of holes someone had dug as if looking for something. She scowled, knowing that the children had most likely been forced to dig them.

As she crested the next hill, her heart nearly flew out of her chest. Lloyd Stout came into view, still mounted on his fine horse. He looked as if he were dressed to go to a business meeting rather than a day in the hills, working. Then again, Anna doubted he did much other than supervise. She could imagine him lounging on a blanket, eating and drinking, while shouting orders to the poor children, forced to do his bidding.

Her fist tightened around the reins. Mr. Stout motioned to his right and dismounted. Anna backed Bella up and secured her in a small ravine off the trail, then made her way toward the sound of plinking and clunking. She managed to climb up a boulder behind where Mr. Stout had sat down on a big rock shaded by a trio of quaking aspens. The children were spread out in groups of two, one child with a pick and another with a shovel. The bigger child in each group wielded the pick and loosened the hard, rocky soil while the younger one shoveled the dirt.

What were they doing? They had to be searching for something, but what could be buried way out here?

Anna wanted to charge down there and rescue the children this very moment, but she had the sense to know that would be a dumb idea. Lloyd Stout could easily overpower her.

She backed away, knowing if she didn't return to the ranch, Quinn would go looking for her. If she told him what she'd seen, he'd be furious that she'd ridden this far from the Rocking M without a companion. Mounted on Bella, she headed for home. Maybe her best bet would be to tell Brett what she'd seen. He'd know what to do about the situation and wouldn't send her packing to Bismarck like her brother would.

She urged Bella into a gallop, knowing something had to be done for those needy children—and soon.

⁂

Brett carried the two bridles he'd just repaired into the tack room and lit the lantern, illuminating the small area lined with saddles, harnesses, and headgear. Sniffing the scent of leather, an odor he never tired of breathing, he hung up the pair of bridles, proud of the job he'd done repairing them.

He looked around the small room. He'd searched the whole barn, twice, hoping to find a hidey-hole for stolen loot, but he'd come up empty. Bouncing on the boards of the tack room, he looked for a loose one that could be easily pried up. But there were no scratches out of the ordinary, no place to hide anything. Every square inch was used for storing equipment. Latching the door, he turned and faced the house. He needed to get back inside somehow.

"Help me out here, Lord."

The other ranch hands were out rounding up cattle for branding. Though it was autumn, Quinn informed him they generally had a second round of branding. The first round was held in late spring, but this next round was to brand late calves and any new stock they'd accumulated over the summer.

Brett rubbed his chest, hoping he'd be of some help. He hated doing menial jobs but knew his body wasn't yet ready for the more vigorous ranch work. He grabbed a currycomb and brushed the burrs out of Jasper's tail, then his mane. His gelding sniffed his hand, hoping for a treat. "You'd like an apple or carrot, wouldn't you, ol' boy?"

Jasper nickered as if answering and bobbed his head.

"I'd like to just ride out and head home, but I'll always be sorry if I don't finish this job."

But every day that went by, he became less and less certain that the McFarlands were actually the Sallingers. They were just plain too nice to be outlaws. Oh, Quinn could be crotchety, but he was fair and had been extremely patient and had encouraged Brett to not worry about taking it easy until he was totally healed. The two outer scrapes from the bear's claw had healed nicely, but the inner two were deeper and still pained him. How long before he could do a man's full day of work?

He snapped a lead onto Jasper's halter and led his horse outside, setting him loose in a small pasture with plenty of grass to feed on. His gelding bucked and leaped like a young colt, happy to be freed of the confines of his stall. Warm sunshine battled with the light chill, promising a glorious day.

Brett leaned his arms on the fence railing, watching as Jasper settled and ducked his head to graze. He twisted the lead rope in his hand. He had to get back to his own ranch before winter set in. There was so much that needed doing, unless the hands had been diligent to keep the place going. But with Taylor gone, Brett had no idea if the hands had absconded with his cattle or not. How long would a man continue working when nobody was paying him? How loyal were the men to Taylor?

He didn't have a lot of money but had saved most of what he'd earned—and he still had that bank draft for the cattle. Hopefully, that would keep the ranch running for a while. He needed to write to the foreman and let the man know he intended to pay everyone as soon as possible.

Hoofbeats drew his attention back to the present, and he turned around. Lottie rode in on Bella, pulling the mare to a stop just outside the barn. The woman sat a horse well and rode like she'd been doing it all her life. A wide smile brightened her face, and the sun gleamed off the yellow braid hanging down her back. Why couldn't she be as ugly as three-day-old stew and as mean as a cougar?

It would sure make things easier for him. Sighing, he walked toward her and held Bella's bridle as Lottie dismounted.

"Fine day for riding." Lottie smiled and patted her horse on the neck.

"Yep, it is." Brett led Bella into the barn, hoping Lottie wouldn't follow. He put the horse in her stall and swapped the bridle for a halter, then gave her a bucket of feed. Lottie followed and uncinched the saddle. She started to tug it off, but Brett reached for it.

"I'll get it." His hand landed on top of Lottie's, and his gaze met hers. He should move away, but his feet were stuck, as if trapped in quicksand.

"Uh. . .thanks." Cheeks flaming, Lottie tugged her hand free and picked up a brush.

Brett ducked his head, certain that his ears matched her red cheeks. What was he thinking, staring at Lottie like that? The problem was, he enjoyed working side by side with her. What would it be like to do that every day? To wake up beside her? To hold her close each morning?

Brett wished for a bucket of cold water to douse his head in. He yanked off the saddle. The only way he and Lottie would ever be together was if he joined her in a jail cell.

He kicked open the tack room door and slung the saddle onto the block where it belonged. This room reminded him of the one on his own ranch. Tending tack had always been something he found rewarding. Well-cared-for leather would last years longer than if it was neglected. Was his ranch being neglected?

Lottie cleared her throat, and he turned. She leaned against the doorjamb, blocking his exit. "I have a confession. I didn't just go riding; I went back to the orphanage."

Clenching his teeth, Brett glared at her. "You're not supposed to go there alone."

She shrugged. "I told you I could take care of myself." Her high-minded attitude seemed to shift as her expression softened. "Oh, Brett. You should have seen those poor children. That man has them digging all day, hunting for something."

Thoughts swirled in his mind. "I wonder what he thinks is out there."

"I don't know, but we've got to find out."

Brett shook his head. "It won't happen any time soon. We

leave for roundup today. You know that."

Lottie crossed her arms and kicked at a tuft of hay. "I can't stand the thought of those children hurting and us not doing anything."

"I know." He stepped toward her, wishing he could offer more comfort than mere words.

"Maybe I shouldn't go on the roundup and instead ride into town and talk to the sheriff."

Brett took hold of her upper arms, drawing her gaze to his. "You'll do no such thing. Lloyd Stout could be dangerous. He obviously doesn't mind hurting innocents. Just what do you think he'd do to a beautiful woman, off all by herself? You'll go on the roundup, just like I will, and when we get back, we'll think up a way to help the children."

She glared at him, jerked away, and stomped out of the barn. Maybe he should say something to Quinn about his sister and her foolish notions. He shook his head. The boss was busy enough with getting things ready for a three-day roundup. Brett would just have to keep his eye on Lottie and make sure she didn't do anything else stupid.

As he brushed Bella down, his thoughts returned to the Bar W and all of the memories he'd made there—some good, some not so good. What would be the point of having such a place with no family to share it with?

Maybe he ought to just sell it. If he couldn't share it with the woman of his choosing, the Bar W would be a lonely place.

Brett shook his head, trying to dislodge the thought of Lottie living at the Bar W with him. Maybe that hit on his head during the bear attack had done more damage than he'd realized.

thirteen

Brett lounged against a downed tree and studied the flickering campfire. His body cried out for rest after three days of herding cattle and branding. In the morning, they'd be leaving these hills and going back home. No, not home, just back to the bunkhouse—or cabin, in Jack and Lottie's case.

Lottie stood beside her brother, laughing at something he'd said. She looked tired but exhilarated. At first, he'd been worried about her riding among the herd and doing a man's job, but she'd proved herself more than capable with her expert roping and even wielding a hot brand like a cowpoke. Sleeping outside didn't even appear to bother her. She would make the perfect rancher's wife, if only. . .

Why would Jack allow her to live among the ranch hands like this and to risk her life cutting cantankerous cattle from the herd? Brett didn't like the protectiveness surging through him. Was he just trying to protect her so that he could see justice done? Or were his feelings more personal?

Getting emotionally involved would only make his job harder.

Brett nodded his thanks as Cookie handed him a plate of stew and biscuits. His mouth watered as he took a bite of the still-warm bread.

Claude, the old-timer, eased down onto the trunk next to Brett. "Whew, long day, huh?"

Brett nodded, wondering how the man had lasted all day. Quinn had wanted to leave him at home, but Claude had insisted he still had it in him to do one more roundup.

"These old bones ain't what they used to be. Let me tell

you, son, enjoy life while you're young. Don't end up an old codger with no place of your own." He shoved a spoonful of stew into his mouth. "Now don't get me wrong, I love it here, but a young fellow like you should dream bigger than working for someone else all his life."

Brett contemplated Claude's words. The man couldn't know he'd been considering selling his ranch. Was this God's way of telling him he was wrong to go down that path?

"If you could do life over, would you change things?"

Claude wheezed a laugh. "I reckon most of us would. But it took a lot of hard livin' and getting rid of stubbornness to get me where I am today—and I don't mean here on the Rocking M, but right with God. I was a fool when I was younger. Thought I was smarter than everyone else, but now I know better."

Brett finished his stew then sopped up the remaining broth with his last biscuit. He needed to pray about the ranch. If he kept it, he'd always have a home. He'd lived on the range for the last five years, and while it was all right for a man his age, he couldn't see living that vagabond life the rest of his days. He wanted to settle. He wanted to go home.

Standing, he stretched and looked at Claude. "Thanks for the advice."

The old-timer's faded blue eyes twinkled, and he nodded. "Glad to be of help."

Brett dropped his tin plate in the pile of dirty ones and decided to stretch his legs before turning in. He checked on Jasper and gave the horse a brisk pat before heading out of camp. Stones clattered behind him, and his hand instinctively reached for his pistol as he spun around. The light from the campfire illuminated a person's silhouette. A woman's silhouette.

Lottie held up her hands. "Whoa, don't shoot me, cowboy."

Humor laced her words.

Brett relaxed, glad that the darkness shielded his embarrassment at overreacting. "Sorry."

"Mind if I walk with you?" She eased up beside him.

How could he explain that the last thing he wanted was to be alone with her in the dark?

"If you want."

They walked in silence for a short ways, the moonlight casting its faint glow on the rocky ground. Beside him, Lottie stumbled, and he grabbed for her.

"Thanks. Mind if I just hold on to your arm? It's harder to see out here than I'd expected."

Yes, he minded, but he couldn't very well tell her that. "Sure. Go ahead."

She looped her arm through his, and Brett clenched his teeth at the sparks shooting through him. *Lord, help me to not be attracted to Lottie.*

"The roundup's gone well. I sure will be glad to sleep in my own bed though." Lottie giggled, a very pleasant sound to Brett's ears.

"You sure handled yourself well out here. I didn't know you were such a cowgirl."

"There are lots of things you don't know about me. And thanks for the compliment."

He knew she was an outlaw. What would she say if he told her that?

"Don't forget I lived over half my life in Texas. I grew up riding and chasing cattle."

"What did your mom think of that?"

"She tried to make me act more like a girl, but with two brothers, it wasn't easy. I wanted to be just like them and my pa. Besides, Ma's not a half-bad cowgirl herself."

Brett figured if they kept talking he would forget about her clinging to his arm and what her closeness did to him. "How did your father die?"

Lottie tsk-tsked, much like he'd heard Leyna do. Brett grinned in the dark.

"It was a terrible accident. He was returning home when a big storm hit. Rain turned to ice and made the trail slick. We think his heavily loaded wagon must have slipped off the edge of the trail where there's a steep drop-off. We found his body and the smashed wagon and dead horses the next day."

"I'm sorry about that. Must have been quite a shock." Brett laid his free hand over hers.

"It was. I can still remember it. Adam and I were just fourteen. Adam took it really hard. In fact, we just found out last year that he blamed himself."

Brett stopped walking. "Why?"

"Pa had told him to replace one of the wagon wheels that was cracked. Adam was sketching that morning and got caught up in his drawing and didn't change it. All that time he'd blamed himself, even to the extent that he quit drawing for many years."

"But it wasn't his fault, was it?"

Brett felt Lottie's arm lift and drop as she shrugged. "I don't think so. How could we ever know for sure? Nobody blames him. It was just an unfortunate accident."

"I understand now why Quinn is so protective of you."

Anna heaved a sigh. "I'll probably end up an old maid because he won't let any man get close enough to get to know me."

Brett couldn't help noticing how close *he* was to her. Was Jack aware that his ranch hand—a U.S. marshal, at that—was walking with his sister in the dark? He couldn't help smiling at the irony of it all. Yes sirree, he'd captured Lottie Sallinger without as much as a fuss. The problem was. . .she had captured his heart. He swallowed the lump in his throat.

Of course, he had no proof he was a marshal, not without his badge. He'd been meaning to go search for it along the creek bed where the bear attack had occurred, but he hadn't been able to get away yet.

"So what are we going to do about the orphans?"

Brett halted and turned to face her. His shadow blocked the moon's light from her face, so he took a step sideways. "Tell me again what you saw."

"Oh, Brett. It was awful. That scoundrel has those poor children digging in the dirt all day, looking for something."

"Did you tell your brother what you saw?"

She shook her head. "He's been too busy with the roundup. I can't sleep at night thinking about how awful things are for the orphans. I've got to do something. I can't let them keep suffering."

She clutched his forearms. "They were digging with shovels—barefoot. Can you imagine how that must hurt?"

Her concern for the youngsters about did him in. He wanted to pull her into his arms and comfort her. "I knew something wasn't right there."

"Stout is using them like prisoners."

"Listen to me. I don't want you going there alone again. If you have to go, I'll go with you."

"What about Quinn and your job here?"

"I'll quit my job if I have to."

Anna smiled, looking up at him with those big brown eyes as if he were her hero. The light breeze whipped a strand of spun gold across her cheek. His mouth went dry, and he forced himself not to look at her lips. Oh, brother, was he in hot water.

❧

Anna couldn't help smiling at Brett's protectiveness. Why, he sounded as if he really cared for her. If only he'd kiss her. . .

But something was holding him back.

"What do you think they could be searching for?"

Brett shrugged. "I have no idea."

"That area is rugged. As far as I know, nobody has ever lived there."

Brett suddenly let go of her arm and snapped his fingers. "I know! I heard mention in town of a payroll shipment that some outlaws had buried in the Badlands around Medora. That must be what they're hunting."

Anna gasped. "I bet you're right. What else could it be?"

"I need to see for myself. I'll ride out at dawn the day after tomorrow if things work out and follow them like you did."

"I'll go with you."

"No, you stay at home." Brett laid his hands on her shoulders and tightened his grasp as if he meant business.

"You can't force me to stay home. Besides, how will you explain your being gone to Quinn?"

Brett remained silent. Anna wished she could see his face, but his back was to the moon. At dinner, she'd watched him across the campfire. He looked even more handsome with stubble darkening his jaw and his face tanned from the sun. Her stomach had done funny things, as if there were critters in there turning somersaults. Was she falling in love? Is that why she tingled all over whenever he touched her?

"I'll tell Quinn I want to ride out and watch the sunrise and want you to escort me—and we *will* watch it, so I'll be telling the truth. All right?"

Brett rolled his head, trying to work the tension out of his neck. "I guess that would work, but I want you to stay back if things go bad."

"What do you intend to do?"

"Nothing yet. I want to see what's going on. Then I'll go to the sheriff."

"Thank you, Brett. It means so much to me that you're

willing to risk your job to help those orphans."

Before she considered her actions, she stepped on her tiptoes and kissed him on the cheek. His stubble pricked her lips, or maybe that was the fire she felt ignited within herself. Anna turned and hurried back to camp, afraid to see Brett's response.

fourteen

The morning after they'd all returned from roundup, Brett and Lottie lay side by side on their stomachs on the bluff overlooking the orphanage, after watching a glorious sunrise. There was no movement below, but the occasional shout of a child could be heard. A dozen chickens roamed about in a small pen behind the house, and a goat was tethered to a cottonwood tree, with its twin kids butting heads and frolicking around her. One goat was hardly enough to provide milk for so many children. Brett's ire rose at Lloyd Stout—or maybe he was still angry with himself.

The cold boulder, not yet warmed from the sun's touch, chilled his bones. Maybe he was still upset with himself over his lack of response to Lottie's kiss. Why hadn't he stopped her? Told her it couldn't happen again?

It had been an impulse on her part, he was sure of that. He could tell she was embarrassed. She hadn't looked at him once they returned to camp, and she'd avoided him most of yesterday. 'Course, he'd been busy, helping to unload the chuck wagon and assisting Cookie in putting things away. And all the time he'd worked, he'd thought of Lottie.

He slid a glance her way. The sun glimmered on her hair like pure gold. He wanted to reach out and touch it, feel its softness. Gazing at her profile, he noticed for the first time that her pert nose turned up the tiniest bit at the end. Her thin brows matched her hair, and her appealing lips were pressed together.

He forced his attention back to the house. He was a goner. He'd stayed too long at the Rocking M, and now his mind would need a good scrubbing to rid its chambers of Lottie.

He'd heard of other lawmen falling for one of their captives, but he never would have believed it could happen to him. Gazing up at the sky, he made another appeal for help. *C'mon, Lord. I need to find evidence of that bank robbery, so I can finish this job and get on home. I've drawn a blank so far. You've gotta help. I can't act on my attraction to Lottie. It's wrong.*

Good thing he was quitting the U.S. Marshals after this. If a woman could get under his skin like Lottie had, he was better off staying on his ranch, herding cattle rather than chasing outlaws. A man with his attention divided could get himself—or someone else—killed.

"Look!" Lottie hissed and scooted closer. "I told you so."

Brett watched a half-grown boy come out of the house and enter a lean-to. He tossed out a mixture of picks and shovels. Another boy, smaller than the first, went inside the rickety barn and soon returned with Stout's saddled horse.

One by one, children came dragging out of the house, rummaged through the tools, and took one. A trio of girls headed to the privy, while the other children stood or sat on the ground. Lloyd Stout ventured out last, stretching and patting his oversize belly. It took him three tries before he managed to mount the horse.

Brett prayed he'd see enough today to have the man behind bars by tonight—as long as the sheriff wasn't in cahoots with Stout.

Lottie started to rise, but Brett threw his arm over her. "Stay down. They can see us too easily."

She looked at him with wide brown eyes. "They never saw me last time."

Stubborn woman. He needed to withdraw his arm but feared she'd get up again. Lottie turned her head to watch something to her right and her warm breath teased his cheek. How could holding her feel so right when he knew it was wrong?

If truth be told, he'd wanted to pull her in his arms the other night and kiss her. Would she have welcomed his kiss? Somehow he thought she might.

The children lined up and followed Lloyd Stout up a path and then disappeared from sight. Brett couldn't decide whether to follow on foot or horseback.

"Can I get up now? They're gone."

Brett peered over at Lottie. Her face was only a foot away. All he had to do was lean a bit. . .

"Get up, Brett. We don't want them to get away. They might not be going to the same place I saw them go the other day." Lottie squirmed until he rolled away.

Brett shook his head and jumped up. Being alone with Lottie was getting dangerous. They moved back from the edge of the butte and hurried back to the horses.

"I think we should ride instead of walking. They went over a mile the last time I watched them." Lottie mounted without waiting for a response. She nudged Bella forward.

Brett shook his head. "Let me go first."

Lottie sighed but waited. "Why do men always have to go first?"

Brett grinned. "So we can protect you, princess."

❧

Anna's breath caught in her throat at the endearment. But did it mean anything to him?

The ranch hands had often called her endearing names, especially when she was younger, but Brett never had. And why "princess"? Did he think she was spoiled? Adam had called her that a time or two when teasing her, but hadn't she shown Brett she was willing to get dirty to help the orphans? Didn't she pull her weight on the roundup?

Anna pressed her lips together. At some point her feelings for Brett had sprouted from admiration to love. But loving a cowhand was a waste of time. Quinn would never allow them to court, much less marry, even if Brett desired that also. If her brother even suspected there was an attraction growing between them, he'd never let Brett escort her anywhere again.

She leaned back in the saddle, stirrups forward as Bella descended to the valley floor. Brett glanced back at her, probably wanting to be sure she'd made it down the steep hill. She wasn't a baby. Couldn't he see she was a woman well past marrying age? And she was interested in him.

He slowed his horse as he rounded the bend then urged him around the corner. Anna followed. This time the children took a different trail, but their tracks were just as easy to see as before. Half an hour later, she followed Brett as he crawled out on another butte and looked down. A muscle in his jaw clenched.

"It's the same as before," Anna whispered. "The bigger kid works the pick, and the younger one shovels the dirt. They're looking for something. That's obvious."

Stout sat atop his horse, riding from one hole to another. "Dig it deeper. You ain't gonna find nothing in the topsoil."

"Just look at him," Anna whispered, "dressed in his nice clothes and riding that fine horse while those poor children do manual labor. If I weren't a God-fearing woman. . ."

"Shh."

"Are you going to do anything? Those children have suffered long enough."

Brett clenched his fist and scowled. "I'm thinking on it. I don't want the kids to get hurt."

One girl, who looked to be nine or ten, stood and pressed her hands into her back after wielding the heavy pick. Her gaze landed on Brett and Anna, and her eyes widened. She glanced at Mr. Stout and then went back to work.

Anna rushed backward, sending pebbles clattering off the edge of the butte. Brett jumped back. She rubbed her hands together and wiped the dirt off her jacket and riding skirt.

"You think Mr. Stout saw us?" Anna asked as she hurried toward Bella.

"Don't think so." Brett followed her.

"So. . .did you see enough?"

His angry glare made her want to never get on his bad side. "Yes. I need to get to town and tell the sheriff what I saw."

"All right, then. Let's go."

Excitement surged through Anna like a flash flood. For the first time in her life, she felt she might actually make a difference in someone's life.

⚈

Brett watched Lottie dismount and march into the sheriff's office without even waiting on him. Again, it struck him odd how an outlaw could have the audacity to enter a sheriff's domain without a speck of apprehension. Either she was very certain of her disguise as Anna McFarland, or she wasn't the woman he thought she was. And he was wondering that more and more, and hoping it also. Why, if Anna truly wasn't Lottie Sallinger. . .

His heart soared at the possibilities. But he had that drawing in his pocket. And no evidence. How long should he keep looking?

He dismounted, looped his reins over the hitching post, and followed Lottie into the office. She was already halfway through her spiel, like a country peddler. The sheriff's gaze darted to Brett and back to Lottie. She finally ran out of steam.

"So, you see, we've got to do something to save those children."

Sheriff Jones scratched his jaw. "Those folks tend to stay to themselves up there. I've been a bit suspicious of that place, but I don't know that any laws have been broken. Not sure what I can do."

"You can protect those orphans. He's mistreating them.

Why, they don't even go to school." Lottie hiked her chin and shoved her hands to her slim waist.

"Tell me what you saw." The sheriff turned to Brett.

"Same as she did. Stout dressed in his fancy clothes, riding a well-fed buckskin, and those barefoot kids digging in the dirt with picks and shovels. We saw the home, too. The kids don't have decent clothes, and some of the smaller kids had runny noses. The law should protect such little ones."

"There's no law about kids having to go to school, but I've gotten a notice or two about children gone missing around Bismarck and Mandan. A boy was found wandering the hills around the Circle G Ranch last month, but he didn't fit the description of any of those lost children. He was sickly and didn't know his name or how he came about getting lost. After the doc treated him, I took him out to the orphanage. I was grateful they took him in, even though the place is kind of rough looking. Guess I could ride out and check up on the boy and have a look around."

Brett leaned against the wall of the small office. "I have a theory. I think Stout's looking for that lost gold shipment that's rumored to be hidden in the hills."

The sheriff twisted the end of his mustache. "You know, you might be right. I bet that *is* what they're doing."

"That money belongs to the railroad. I'm sure there's a reward for it."

Lottie tossed her arms up. "Who cares about money when children are suffering? If you're not going to do anything, I will."

She turned and strode toward the door. Brett blocked her way. "You're not going there alone."

"You two are just yakking while the orphans are killing themselves doing a grown man's job." Tears glistened in her eyes. She was really taking this whole thing quite seriously for someone who held up a bank. Must be that even outlaws had a tender spot—some bigger than others.

He held on to her shoulders. "We'll take care of this. Right, Sheriff?"

The man held Brett's gaze and nodded. "Tonight. After dinner, when we're sure the children are at home. I don't want any of them getting hurt if things go bad."

fifteen

"So, what should we do now?" Anna stood outside the sheriff's office; fingers of the morning sun touched her face. "We can't stay in town all day."

Brett stretched. "Don't know about you, but I'm hungry. How about we eat some breakfast and then decide what to do?"

Anna nodded and walked beside Brett on the boardwalk. The sleepy town of Medora was barely awake, and only a handful of other people were out and about. Brett's stomach growled, and he wondered what the orphans had eaten for breakfast.

After a heaping plate of fried ham, eggs, biscuits, and gravy, Brett leaned back in his chair, sipping his coffee. He watched Lottie swipe the napkin across her mouth and held back a grin. She wasn't the most dainty of women; in fact, when she was in a hurry to get somewhere, she tended to swagger like a man. Could be because of that split skirt she insisted on wearing so often. And he'd seen her jump clear off the porch without even using the steps a time or two when she thought nobody was watching.

"So. . .what do you plan to do with the rest of your life?"

Her eyes widened at his pointed question. She shrugged. "I don't know. I guess I want what most women do—to marry the man of my dreams and raise a family. It would also be nice if I didn't have to cook."

Brett couldn't help smiling at that. "You don't like to cook?"

She glanced away, a pleasant pink blush on her cheeks. "I can fix a few things, but haven't really had to cook since Leyna came to live with us. I'd much rather be helping with the horses—at least I used to be satisfied with that."

"And you dream about men?"

"What?" Her gaze zipped in his direction.

"You said you wanted to marry the man of your dreams, so I just figured you must be dreaming about someone."

Her cheeks flamed, and her gaze flittered around the room like a hummingbird dashing from flower to flower. "I'd rather not talk about that."

What would cause such a reaction? Unless she was dreaming about. . .

No. He couldn't allow himself to think that. It wasn't fair to her—or to him.

Lottie nibbled her lip, as if she were preparing to tell him a deep secret. She glanced at him and cocked her head. "Lately, I've been dissatisfied. Feeling the need to do more with my life."

"I understand. That's how I felt when I left home and became a. . ." Brett choked on his almost revelation that he was a lawman. He picked up his coffee and took a gulp.

Lottie leaned forward. "Became a what?"

He studied the other people in the room, hoping Lottie wouldn't press him further. A couple, two tables over, sat cramming food into their mouths as if they hadn't eaten in weeks. Two women dressed in calico chatted amiably over their coffee and cinnamon rolls. Silverware clinked, and the aroma of fresh cooked food filled the air, but it didn't smell as good to him now as when he'd first come in.

Lottie touched his arm, drawing his attention back to her. "Became a what?"

"Uh. . .guess you could say I'm a drifter. Traveling from place to place."

Lottie smiled and ran her finger around the top of her coffee mug. "Sounds interesting to me. That's kind of what Adam and Mariah do. I've often dreamed of traveling like that. It must be wonderful to see so many different sights instead of being stuck on a ranch all the time."

Brett swallowed hard. "So you don't have any desire to marry a rancher?"

"No. Never."

He flinched at her adamant response. That certainly made things easier. Not that he ever would have asked her to marry him, but knowing she didn't want to marry a rancher eliminated him. So why didn't he feel relieved?

"I guess I shouldn't say never." Lottie's lips tilted in a melancholy smile. "If I loved a man who was a rancher, I think I'd enjoy living on *his* ranch, seeing him daily, waiting for him to come home in the evenings. Life wouldn't be so lonely if you were with the one you loved."

Brett's throat tightened. She looked at him—almost as if she loved him. But it couldn't be. He couldn't allow it. Standing, he fished some coins out of his pocket. "We'd best get back to the ranch."

"You're right. I need to explain everything to Quinn. If the Stouts leave, I may have to stay with the children until we can find a new overseer."

"You gonna cook for them?" He couldn't help the ornery gleam in his eye as he held open the café door for her.

"Ha-ha." Anna stuck her tongue out at him, right there on Main Street. "Maybe I'll let you do the cooking."

He chuckled as he mounted Jasper. "I need to see if I have any mail since we're in town."

"That's fine. I want to check at the mercantile and see if they have enough clothes in stock so I can buy a set for each child. They need something now, and it will take too long to hear back from my grandma."

"Don't you need to check with Quinn before spending so much money?" He clicked out the side of his mouth, and Jasper moved forward.

Lottie tossed her head like a wild mustang. "The Rocking M is just as much mine as it is his, I'll have you know. Pa's will left Mama one-fourth of the ranch and each of us three kids one-fourth."

Brett knew when to keep quiet. He just shook his head and reined Jasper toward the post office, thinking what a woman that Lottie Sallinger was.

Disappointment resurfaced when he discovered he still hadn't heard from Marshal Cronan. He was just about ready to cut his losses and leave town. The more he was around Lottie, the less he believed she was an outlaw. There had to have been a mistake.

He leaned against a post outside the mercantile and watched the people ambling up and down the dirt road and boardwalks. There were more people here today than usual, probably because the train had arrived while they were eating. A pretty blond woman who looked to be in her forties stopped across the street and looked in the window of the dress shop. There was something oddly familiar about her.

She slowly turned, and Brett's heart stumbled. Why, the woman looked just like Lottie, only older. The woman looked both directions then crossed the street after a buggy passed.

"There you are." Lottie exited the store and stopped beside him. "What's wrong? You look like you've seen a ghost."

He nudged his chin toward the woman, and Lottie turned. "Mama? Oh, my goodness—" She glanced back at Brett. "Is it Friday already? How could I have not realized today is Friday?"

She tossed a small package into his arms and jumped off the steps, meeting her mother in the street. "I'm so sorry we didn't meet you at the train. We had roundup this week, and I completely lost track of what day this was."

Her mother hugged her again. "It's all right, darling. I was just about to go to the livery and rent a buggy, but I thought

I'd find something to drink first."

"There's a bucket and a dipper in the mercantile, or we could go to the café if you're hungry."

They walked arm in arm toward Brett. He looked back and forth, amazed at their similarities. Lottie was an inch taller than her ma, but they could almost be twins. Now that he thought about it, her mother must have been the woman he'd seen her with in Bismarck that first day. He'd just been too focused on Lottie to pay any attention to her companion.

"There's someone I want you to meet." She pointed to Brett. "This is the man who saved me from the bear."

Mrs. McFarland started up the steps, and Brett reached out to assist her. She took his hand then held it between both of her hands once she was on the boardwalk. "I owe you a great debt, Mr. . .uh. . ."

"Wickham," Brett and Lottie said in unison, and Mrs. McFarland joined them in a chuckle.

"Thank you for rescuing my half-wild daughter. You can't know how much that means to me."

Brett swallowed, wondering what she'd say if she knew that he had planned to arrest her son and daughter. "Uh. . .you're welcome, ma'am. I was happy to do it."

"You should see his scars, Mama, from where the bear clawed his chest."

Mrs. McFarland lifted one brow. "And you *shouldn't* be seeing them, young lady."

Lottie waved her hand in the air. "I see the men's chests all the time in warm weather. What's one more?"

Mrs. McFarland shook her head. "You see, Mr. Wickham, I've raised a hooligan."

His grin turned into a scowl as Lottie and her mother entered the mercantile. He liked the woman—but he didn't want to. It only made his job harder. Was she also involved? Hadn't she been living in Bismarck for over a year? Could be she was innocent and unaware of her son and daughter's misdeeds.

One thing for sure, his job just got more complicated.

❦

"Whoa!" Lottie stopped the wagon loaded with clothes and supplies for the children just before rounding the final bend to the orphanage. "What now?"

Brett glanced at Sheriff Jones and his deputy, Chester Brennan. "How are we gonna play this out?"

The sheriff leaned on his saddle horn and scratched his bristly chin. "I don't imagine Lloyd Stout will go easily. I can't say he's done anything illegal, but folks around here won't like him taking advantage of children. I think if we rattle him enough, he'll ride out of town of his own free will."

"And what if he doesn't?"

The sheriff sighed. "Don't know. I couldn't find any laws against child labor in this state. Maybe if we could prove he was guilty of using donations for himself instead of the children. . ." He shrugged one shoulder.

"Well then, we will pray that he takes the hints and leaves." Ellen McFarland had insisted on coming with Lottie when she learned what was happening tonight. She had been adamant about not allowing her daughter to stay overnight alone at the orphanage.

Lottie hadn't taken too well to her wings of independence being clipped so quickly and so efficiently. Brett had heard them arguing clear outside. Jack had even considered riding along, but Lottie had told him everything was under control.

"Let's do this. Chester and I will go to the front door. You reckon you could cover the back in case Stout tries to sneak out?" The sheriff eyed Brett as if taking his measure.

"Yes, sir. I can do that."

"All right. We'll leave the horses here and go in quietly. Maybe take Stout by surprise. I don't want any of them youngsters getting hurt. You women stay here."

Lottie scowled at being left out, and Brett couldn't help grinning. He tipped his hat and winked at her then followed the two lawmen. He felt good being back in action, even if it was unofficially. Sheriff Jones and Deputy Brennan walked along the side of the house and onto the porch. Brett heard their solid knock as he walked behind the house.

Three children were batting small rocks around with sticks. Their eyes widened at his approach. Brett held up his finger and motioned to them to move away from the house. One child dropped her stick and raced into the rickety barn with the other two close on her heels. Brett heaved a sigh of relief to have them safe and out of the way, but he didn't like thinking that he might have frightened them. And where were the other children? Around the dinner table, he hoped.

"Who do you think you are to come here and tell me what I can or can't do?" Brett recognized Lloyd Stout's voice from when he'd hollered at the children while Brett and Lottie had spied on him. The murmur of the sheriff's voice echoed along the walls of the house, but he couldn't make out the softer words.

"That's ridiculous. I took these snotty-nosed kids in when nobody else wanted them, but I'm not going to jail for them."

Brett wondered what the sheriff had said to get such a reaction from Stout. There may be no laws to protect children, but Stout didn't necessarily know that. Maybe with enough pressure he'd just leave, but that always meant he could sneak back. The children might never be safe from him.

He heard a ruckus and heavy steps running through the house, and he peered around the corner.

"No, Lloyd, don't leave me here with them."

"Turn loose of me, woman," Stout hollered, and the sound of banging furniture echoed out the back door. Brett imagined that Stout had shoved his sister aside so he could get away. Brett's dislike for the man grew by the second.

The sheriff came around the front side of the house, his nose bloody, just as Stout burst out the back door waving a pistol. Brett couldn't fire without risk of hitting the sheriff and deputy. He hugged the house, and a second later Stout rounded the corner.

Brett let his fist fly in the face of the surprised man. Stout grabbed his bleeding nose, but before Brett could react, Stout elbowed him hard in the chest, right where the bear had clawed him. He doubled over, clutching his chest and gasping for a breath free of pain. Stout lumbered around the boulders toward where the women were waiting. *No!*

The sheriff and his deputy glanced at Brett but rushed past him. Ignoring the inferno in his torso, he jogged after them, hoping Stout hadn't harmed one of the women. As he rounded the corner, he skidded to a halt at the sheriff's deep, rumbling chuckle.

Lottie stood in the wagon, holding a rifle on Stout. "Go ahead and move. After the way you've treated those children, jail is too good for you." Lloyd Stout held one hand on his bloody nose and the other in the air and glanced back as if he hoped the sheriff would rescue him.

Brett grinned. *Good job, Lottie!*

The sheriff hauled Stout, whimpering and complaining, back toward the house. "It may not be illegal to force children to work all day in unseemly conditions, but it is against the law to assault a sheriff. You're going to jail, Mister."

The children came out of the house, the bigger ones first, followed by the younger. They huddled in a group and watched, wide-eyed. Deputy Brennan saddled Stout's horse and Lloyd mounted, holding a handkerchief to his face.

"I don't know what's to become of me. Will I go to jail, too, Lloyd?" Hattie wrung her hands around a small satchel and gazed up at her brother.

"Just hush, Hattie, and get on." He held out his hand, and

the woman managed to clamber up behind him.

The sheriff stopped in front of Brett as Lottie and her mother pulled up in the wagon. "Thanks for alerting me to this and helping in the capture."

Brett nodded. But he really hadn't done all that much. Stout had sucker punched him and slipped past. Brett studied the ground. He was getting too old for chasing outlaws and the like.

Jimmy stepped out of the crowd, followed by Emma. Both children's faces were filthy, as was their ragged clothing. Never had he known the lack they had. "What's gonna happen to us? Are we going to jail, too?"

Emma's chin quivered, and Brett stooped down in front of her and her brother. "No, pardner. You did nothing wrong, but Mr. Stout *is* going to jail for being cruel to you."

Emma nodded. "Good. Him's a bad man."

Brett smiled and tousled her hair. "Yes, he is. And he won't be hurting you again. In fact, I brought two women who will take care of you tonight—and I do believe they have some gifts for you."

The children's gaze turned as one toward the wagon. For the first time since Brett had seen these youngsters, hope brightened their eyes. He rubbed his chest, aching both from the blow he'd taken and from the mistreatment the orphans had endured. Why was it that some people had so much and others so little?

sixteen

Anna swiped her arm across her sweaty forehead. She and her mom had made several trips to the nearby creek, taking first the girls to bathe, and then the infant boy. Brett oversaw the older boys, making sure they didn't shirk in their washing.

The orphanage sounded like the McFarland home used to when they'd open presents on Christmas morning, back in Texas when they were young.

"I got a red shirt and new pants!" a cute boy with a freckled nose declared.

"Mine's blue and matches my britches." Jimmy ran his hand proudly down the front of his new top.

The girls, ages three to nine, twirled around and admired each other's dresses. Brett leaned against the door frame, arms crossed and a gentle smile on his handsome face. He looked as pleased as she felt. Her heart danced with. . .love. Was that what she felt? Did she love him? Or did she just admire him for the way he helped make sure that evil man could no longer harm these children?

Her mother plaited Junie's hair then tied a bow on each short braid. She looked over the child's head and smiled. "There you go, sweetheart."

Junie spun around to face Anna's mother. "Are you my new mommy?"

Anna's heart nearly melted. Her mother touched Junie's cheek. "No, darling, I'm just here to help take care of you for a while."

Junie ducked her head. "I want you to stay. You's nicer than them other folks."

Ellen hugged the girl and wiped a tear from her cheek. Anna wrestled with her thoughts. How could a loving God allow children to be mistreated so?

Brett went outside and returned a few minutes later carrying two bundles that held the orphans' new nightshirts. Anna hoped the sizes were all right. Some of the clothes she'd picked out had been too big, but the children hadn't seemed to mind.

"Gather round, everyone. We have something else for you." Anna and her mother handed out the nightshirts and instructed the older children to get ready for bed. They helped the younger ones change into their nightclothes.

Suzanne started crying. "I don't wanna give back my new dress. I neber had a new one afore." She wrapped her arms around her chest and clung to the pink garment.

Anna smiled and knelt in front of her. "You don't have to give it back, sugar. It's yours to keep, and you get to keep the nightgown, too." She held out the soft flannel gown.

"Truly?" Suzanne still didn't seem to believe her.

Anna pulled the girl's arms open and placed the nightgown in them. "See, you get both of them. One you wear at night and the other during the day. So. . .are you ready to change now?"

Suzanne nodded; then Anna helped her swap clothes and carried her to bed. She wished she'd had the foresight to think about getting new bedding. The sheets and worn blankets looked as if they hadn't been cleaned in months. Tomorrow they'd stay busy washing it all.

With the children tucked into bed, Anna joined her mother and Brett on the porch. They sat in rockers, resting after their hectic evening. "What do you think will happen to them now? Couldn't we take them home to the Rocking M? There's plenty of room on the ranch for a bunch of children."

Brett's gazed swerved toward her, as did her mother's. "You think you could handle raising eleven children by yourself?"

her mother asked, brows raised like a stern schoolmarm.

Anna shrugged. "I wouldn't be alone. Quinn's there." She glanced at Brett, hoping he would agree to help with the orphans, too.

Her mother shook her head. "You have a big heart, Anna, but those children need to be where they have a chance to be adopted. I know a couple of middle-aged sisters who might be willing to watch the children until we can find another place for them to go or a new person to oversee the orphanage. Do you remember the Allen sisters?"

Anna leaned forward, disappointed that she couldn't keep the children but seeing the practicality in her mother's words. She'd been so certain that God had sent her to the children to help them, but she had, in a small way. Hadn't she?

She did remember the Allen sisters. The younger sister had never married and had come to live with the widowed older sister after her husband died. Both were sweet, kind women who were always cooking and doing for others. They would be perfect, if they could handle eleven children.

Her thoughts swirled in her mind. Yes, things were getting better for the children, but why had they had to endure what they did? "I just don't understand why God didn't help these children."

She sensed Brett's gaze on her and turned toward him. He cocked his head and smiled. "God did help them. He sent you to rescue them."

Anna ducked her head, confused by his piercing stare. "But why didn't He help them sooner? Why did they have to suffer such inhumane treatment?"

Her mother reached out and took her hand. "There will always be cruel people in this world who capitalize off the pain of others. You're not to blame for that."

"I know, but my heart still aches for them. If only I'd known about them sooner."

"We have to trust in God's timing. He sees things we don't." Brett's warm smile touched her being, just like hot coffee on a cold morning. He stood and stretched. "I need to take care of the horses. I'll sleep in the barn, but just holler if you need me."

As he ambled past Anna, he patted her shoulder, sending fingers of fire radiating down her arm. His waffling signs of affection and periods of withdrawal confused her. Why. . .she couldn't even remember a time he had called her by her name, and yet, sometimes his sapphire eyes seemed to brim with affection. What was holding him back? Why did he pull away every time they made an emotional connection?

She glanced at the darkening sky, inky to the east with pink and orange clouds disappearing behind the tall butte to the west. *Lord, You know my struggles. Is Brett the man for me? Please, Father, show me how to reach him. What to say to him.*

With just a little sign of interest on his part, her heart would be his. . .if it wasn't already.

⁂

Brett leaned against the depot wall and watched Lottie wave at her mother and the orphans as the train pulled out of the station, leaving only a smelly cloud of smoke littering the air. The engine wailed out a lonely farewell. Lottie stood with her arms clutched around her middle as if saying good-bye to the children and her mother threatened to squeeze the life out of her.

"It's too bad the Allen sisters felt they were too old to oversee the orphanage." Lottie swiped at a tear.

"At least they offered to help your mother take the youngsters to that children's home in Bismarck." Word had been sent that several of the children might have been kidnapped from local families there and that their parents would be waiting at the depot in hopes of finding their lost offspring.

Lottie dabbed her eyes and sniffed.

Brett handed her his handkerchief. "Are you sad because

your ma is moving permanently to Bismarck or because the orphans are gone?"

"Both, I suppose. I've suspected for a long while that Mama would stay there with Grandma, but I wish she would have let me go and help with the children."

He struggled not to wrap a comforting arm around her shoulders. "She didn't want you to have to travel home alone again."

"I could have come back with the Allen sisters, or you could have come with me."

He shook his head. She was getting too dependent on him, beginning to care too much. He closed his eyes, thinking how hurt she would be when she learned the truth about him—and as much as he despised what she and Jack had done, Brett didn't want to hurt Lottie. Her soft hand squeezed his forearm.

"I know you miss the children, too, but for me, it's different. I was so certain that God had brought them into my life so that I could help them and make a difference in theirs."

"You did. You probably saved their lives. Can't you see that? The whole town was oblivious to what was going on at that place—how those kids were being mistreated. If you hadn't figured it out, they'd still be there, and Stout would still be using them to search for that gold. I think your mother didn't want you to go along because she could see how attached you were getting to the kids and thought it would be easier to say good-bye here."

Her tears were his undoing. A lawman should keep his distance, but he couldn't stand to see her suffering and not offer comfort. "Come here."

She fell into his arms, her tears wetting his chest. She wrapped her arms around him and clung to the back of his shirt. He crushed her in a single hug, knowing this would be the only one he could ever offer her. She filled his being, made him long for things that could never be. In many ways, she was the woman his heart had been searching for, but no matter how much he loved her—and yes, he would admit it this once—she'd never be his.

He loved Anna—not Lottie. It was sweet, caring Anna who had sneaked in and stolen his heart with her gentle spirit and spunky determination. He crushed her to his chest, his head resting against her soft, sweet-smelling hair.

He'd searched the barn and all of the outbuildings several times while the other men were out with the cattle or horses, and he had even managed to look around the house when he brought firewood in to the various rooms. There had been no sign that the McFarlands had ever robbed a bank. Somewhere, somehow there'd been a mistake. The person who'd given Lottie's description must have seen Anna or someone who closely resembled her at some point on the day of the robbery and had her in mind when describing the bank thief to the sketch artist. It was time for him to leave. He slammed the door of his heart and set her away from him, already missing her closeness.

She blinked and stared at him as if she were confused. She heaved a heavy sigh. "Before we return home, I need to purchase a few blankets. We donated all of our spare ones to the orphans, and with winter coming soon, we'll need more."

The arriving crowd of train passengers had mostly dispersed, leaving only two other groups of people still at the depot. The stench of coal still hung in the air as Brett ushered her toward the mercantile. "I need to check at the post office to see if I've gotten any mail."

Lottie smiled. "Would you collect ours, too, if we have any?"

"Sure." He nodded and tried to ignore Lottie's tender gaze. Swallowing hard, he strode to the post office. As soon as he walked in, the clerk shook his head.

"Sorry. I still haven't received any mail for you." He shrugged one shoulder. "Anything else I can do?"

"Yeah, got any mail for the Rocking M?"

The man clad in a white shirt and black pants turned and rummaged through a small stack of letters, pulling out three. "Here you go."

Brett nodded his thanks and pocketed the missives. It was time to send a telegram to the marshal. Hopefully, the clerk was one who could keep his mouth shut. At the telegraph office, Brett penned his message and passed it across the counter. The man scanned the note then glanced up at Brett.

"You a lawman?"

Brett glared at him. "Just read it back to me."

The clerk's gray eyes went wide, and he cleared his throat. "Dead end. Returning soon. Wickham."

"Sounds good. How much do I owe you?"

Brett paid him and left. The sun had crested and was already heading toward the western horizon. They needed to head back to the ranch soon. Brett scratched his chest where the last of the bear gouges was healing over. He'd always have some nasty scars, but they probably wouldn't look too bad once his chest hair finished growing back. He couldn't help smiling when he realized his panic at seeing his bald torso. That rattled him more than his injury had.

Shaking his head, he strode toward the mercantile, knowing it was time he returned to Bismarck. He still had the drawing of Lottie in his pocket, but he no longer believed she and Anna were the same person. Anna. . . A wave of melancholy washed over him. Her name was as pretty as she was.

Brett scowled and refocused. In Bismarck, he would find out the latest news on the Sallingers and then decide what to do. Letting Taylor's murderer run free still rankled him, but he might just have to let God deal with the Sallingers.

He blinked his eyes in the dimmer light of the store and found Lottie—no, Anna—at the counter. Her smile when she saw him sent spirals of awareness swirling in his belly. Maybe there was hope for the two of them one day.

"They only had two blankets, so I ordered the others that we need, as well as a few other things. Might be awhile before they arrive. I hope it won't get too cold before then."

Anna's cloak hung over her arm. Her rose-colored dress swished around her legs when she spun back toward the counter. She'd worn the dress for her mother, but he knew she'd rather be wearing her split skirt. She made a beautiful sight with her hair caught up in that net thing that she'd worn the day he followed her to Medora on the train. He swallowed the lump in his throat. When had he fallen in love with her?

She gathered up the two wool blankets and handed them to him with a sweet smile. His gaze focused on the gold oval necklace with a fancy engraved M that she wore, and a fog blurred his mind. His heart stampeded, knowing the necklace was important. Where had he seen that before?

Anna plunked down two double-eagle gold coins on the counter, and Brett felt the skin on his face tighten. He set the blankets on the counter and picked up one of the coins, not wanting to believe what his eyes were seeing. Running his thumb around, he found the notch that the Northern Pacific treasurer had etched into all the coins in a specific payroll shipment that he had personally delivered to the Bismarck Federal Bank the day before the robbery. The notch rested on the edge of the coin in the space between "twenty" and "dollars," at the bottom of the eagle side of the coin. All of the coins in that specific shipment were dated 1890, just like these. There was no doubt they were from the bank robbery.

Brett felt as if he'd been roped and dragged behind a horse through the Badlands for three days. How could Anna have these particular coins in her possession unless she'd taken part in the robbery?

The store clerk cleared his throat when Brett didn't release the double eagle.

"Is something wrong?" Anna stared up at him, and his gaze dropped to her necklace.

He closed his eyes as he remembered where he'd seen it. A cold numbness wafted over him as his hopes and dreams disappeared like debris in a flash flood. When he opened his eyes, he was a lawman again.

He turned to the clerk. "I'm a U.S. marshal, and these coins were part of a robbery in Bismarck. I'm taking possession of them. They're evidence."

Both the clerk's and Lottie's mouths dropped open.

"What do you mean? Where's your badge?" Lottie stared at him, dumbfounded.

"I lost it when that bear attacked me, but I *am* a marshal." He grabbed the other coin and took Lottie by the arm. She came with no resistance, and for that he was grateful. He didn't want to see her get hurt.

"Wait a minute. What about your order, Miss McFarland?"

Lottie glanced over her shoulder. "Put it on our tab, and I'll pay you next time I'm in town."

She still had no idea of the trouble she was in. Brett gritted his back teeth together. This was the hardest thing he'd ever had to do, except for taking his brother's body to the undertaker.

Lottie pulled at his grasp. "Tell me what's going on, Brett. Where are we going?"

"You'll find out soon enough." He marched her over to the sheriff's office, gaining a few curious glances from passersby. It irked him how Lottie trusted him enough not to question him further. Well. . .she wouldn't trust him much longer, and that thought was worse than the pain of the bear attack.

Sheriff Jones dropped his feet off his desk and smiled when Brett strode in. "Got those youngsters off on the train, did ya? Some of them looked pretty excited."

"I'm here on an altogether different matter." Brett plunked the coins on the sheriff's desk while keeping a tight hold on Lottie.

"What's this?" The sheriff picked up a coin and looked it over.

"I didn't tell you before, because I was working undercover, but I'm a U.S. marshal. Those coins were taken from the Bismarck Federal Bank several weeks back when the Sallingers robbed it. They're marked coins. Railroad officials anticipated a train robbery and marked the coins to make it easier to locate the criminals. The Sallinger Gang had been hitting the trains frequently, and the railroad decided to fight back. It worked because the Sallingers robbed the bank, taking the marked coins."

He shoved Lottie in front of him. "This is Lottie Sallinger."

"What?" Lottie turned her startled gaze on him and tried to jerk her arm out of his hold. "Have you gone crazy?"

The sheriff looked as baffled as she did. "Look here, uh. . . Marshal Wickham, I've known the McFarlands ever since right after they moved here. That there's Anna. She's no criminal."

"I have more evidence." With his free hand, he fished the sketch of Lottie from his pants pocket and handed it to the sheriff.

The man unfolded it and laid the frayed page on his desk. He glanced up from the drawing to Lottie and back down several times. "Well, I'll be. It is her, and she's wearing that same necklace. I'd never have believed it if you hadn't had the picture."

Anna leaned over and stared at the sketch. For the first time, something like panic darkened her gaze. "There's been some mistake. I was at the bank that day, but outside, walking. A female robber ran into me. We both fell down and coins went sailing everywhere. It wasn't until I got home to the

Rocking M that I discovered two coins had fallen into my reticule. Besides, Mother has in her possession a bank draft to replace these coins. Please, Brett, you have to believe me."

She was quick; he'd give her that. His ears were deaf to her pleading, though his heart was another matter. "I need you to lock her up, Sheriff. I have to go after her brother."

Lottie spun around and slapped him on the jaw. Hard. Tears tracked down her cheeks, but she swiped them away. "How could you come into our home and accept our hospitality and then treat us like this? Why. . .I even saved your life."

"Don't forget, I saved yours, too. I have the scars to prove it." He spun back to the sheriff, deadening himself to her pleas. "Will you lock her up? My own brother was killed in that robbery. He was an innocent victim. Help me capture Lottie's brother?"

"I don't see as I have a choice. Come along, little lady." The sheriff took Lottie's arm, and she went without a fight, but the glare she tossed over her shoulder froze Brett down to his toes. The sound of the cell door closing and locking was a death knell in his heart. The only woman he'd ever loved was an outlaw, and she'd never forgive him for what he'd done.

seventeen

Anna sniffed and wiped her eyes again. She kicked and shook the locked door, barely rattling it. Crossing her arms over her chest, she paced the tiny cell, alternating between sobbing from a broken heart to explosive anger at Brett for what he'd done. How could he believe she was an outlaw after he'd gotten to know her and her family? Hadn't he seen their hearts. . .her heart? How she was willing to drop everything to help those poor orphans?

She leaned against the hard wooden wall, refusing to sit on the nasty bed that had held truly vile men. Why, Lloyd Stout had probably been locked up in this very cell and might still be here if the sheriff hadn't sent him on to Dickinson.

Anna kicked her heel against the wall. How could she have not known Brett was a lawman? Even when lying in bed injured there'd been something commanding about him. . . something that drew her like a moth to a lantern.

He was the thief, not her. He'd thoroughly stolen her heart and then tossed her in jail, as if she meant nothing to him. Was he that hardened?

No, she'd touched him, too. She could tell when he held her at the depot. His caress had been that of a man who cared. And hadn't he said his own brother had been killed in the robbery? No wonder he was so determined to find the robbers and convict them. But his craving for justice had blinded him to the truth.

She crossed to one wall, spun around, and crossed back to the other wall. How long would she be locked up here before Quinn learned about it and came to get her? Or would he be imprisoned, too?

Anna blinked as another round of tears threatened. Her heart broke that Brett could think such evil of her. He was the only man she'd ever loved, and now he was dead to her. She leaned her head against the bars with an ache so deep in her heart that she thought it might shatter.

"Oh, Lord. Help me. You know I'm innocent. Please vindicate me. Protect Quinn—and Brett. Don't let them kill each other." Her tears wouldn't stop, and she wiped her nose on her sleeve. The lovely pink dress would be ruined anyway after the filth of the cell. Something skittered along the wall. Anna spun around and jumped back. A mouse!

Desperation drove her on top of the dirty bed. Why did it have to be a mouse? A snake or spider didn't faze her, but ever since she was a child and a mouse had gotten caught under the covers of her bed, she'd been petrified of them. Weak from worry, anger, and now fear, she drew up her legs and leaned against the wall. Elbows on her knees, she rested her head in her hands, covering her face. The stench in the place was horrible. In the adjoining cell, someone had forgotten to empty the chamber pot.

What would happen to her? She'd seen the sketch and had been stunned at how much it resembled her. Even her pendant had been drawn in vivid detail. And with the gold coins as evidence, she stood a good chance of being convicted. Why hadn't she returned the money sooner? The forty-dollar bank draft hadn't even been delivered, since it was just now on its way back to Bismarck in her mother's possession along with a note explaining what had happened. Anna had kept the coins because her mother hadn't wanted to travel with that much money on her.

"Oh, Lord," she sobbed. How would she endure prison? Being locked up, never to ride the valleys and hills of the

Badlands or to feel the sun on her face or the wind blowing her hair?

She gasped. Or would she be hung?

She clutched her throat as her mind raced like a runaway horse. Would she ever see her mother again? Or Adam? Could her twin, wherever he was, sense her distress?

Heedless to her clothing and the mouse, she dropped to her knees. "Heavenly Father, I know I've often been wild and reckless, but I never robbed that bank. You know that. I've never done anything that warranted being locked up like this. Please help me. Help Quinn to evade Brett so he can rescue me."

She wanted to pray that God would punish Brett, but she couldn't. As much as she hurt, she knew he was just trying to do his job—to capture the outlaws who were responsible for his brother's death. The mouse scampered across the floor. Anna jumped up and climbed onto the cot again.

Blinking in the dim lighting, she realized something. The reason Brett had never used her name was probably because he thought of her as Lottie. Now she understood how his moods could change so fast. He had been attracted to her, but he'd been trying to keep his distance.

She wanted to hate him, but she couldn't. Still, it would take a very long time for her wounded heart to trust another man. To love another man.

Anna yawned. She closed her eyes, hoping this was all a bad nightmare, but the stench told her it was real. A fog of sleep descended, taking with it the horrors of the day.

Angry voices pulled Anna from her dreams of riding Bella through the grasslands, and she bolted upright. They echoed through the wall, and the shuffling of footsteps and loud bangs sounded as if men were fighting.

"We're innocent. I've told you that a hundred times."

Quinn! Anna stood and ran her hands down her wrinkled

dress. She wiped her cheeks again. Her brother would have her out in no time.

A key jingled, and the door opened. Brett strong-armed Quinn inside, and the sheriff closed the door, locking it. She couldn't help glancing at Brett. His angered blue gaze softened, then widened. She knew her face was red and splotchy. She couldn't help hoping he'd hurt deeply for what he'd done to her.

"Anna, are you all right?" Quinn took her by the arms and shook her. "Don't look at him. He's the reason we're here."

The outer door closed, taking most of the light with it. Her chin wobbled, but she held back the tears. She wouldn't admit defeat in front of her brother. He'd always thought her a child but she'd prove him wrong. "I'm fine."

Quinn circled the cell, much smaller with his bulky frame in it. "I can't believe this happened. Why did Brett keep calling me Jack?"

"You mean you don't know?" In the shadows, she could see her brother shake his head.

"I was furious when he overpowered me and tied me up. He even got me off the ranch without any of the hands noticing. He's good; I'll give him that. Who would have thought he was a U.S. marshal?"

The smidgen of admiration in Quinn's voice surprised her, knowing her brother's temper. "He's convinced that we're Jack and Lottie Sallinger. They robbed the Bismarck Federal Bank and killed his brother in the process."

Quinn paced back and forth. He ran his hand through his dark blond hair. "But what does that have to do with us?"

"I was there."

Quinn spun to face her; confusion wrinkled his brow. "What?"

"It's not what you're thinking. Mother and I were shopping and decided to get some lunch. She needed to stop at the bank for some more money. Just as I was reaching for the door, a female bank robber—Lottie Sallinger, I'm guessing—charged out the door and ran into me. Her bag of gold coins burst open and went everywhere. I guess two accidentally fell into my bag."

Her brother heaved a heavy sigh that tickled her forehead. "How come you never told me any of this?"

Anna held out her hands. "When would I tell you? You're always working. You never want to talk to me." Her loud shout echoed in the small area. She crossed her arms and turned her back, her gaze landing on the faint light shining in a tiny crack between two boards.

Quinn placed his hands on her shoulders and gently turned her. "I'm sorry, Anna. I know you've been lonely with Adam gone."

"I do miss Adam, but I miss you, too. I love you just as much as Adam."

Quinn pulled her into his arms, and the unwanted tears flowed again.

"I'm sorry. All I know how to do is work. I'm not good with people."

"You are too good with people, or you wouldn't be such a great boss."

He chuckled. "I don't know about that. I promise I'll try to give you more of my time."

"Won't that be difficult if we're in different prisons?" She clutched him tight, remembering how not so long ago Brett had been the one comforting her. Was putting her behind bars hard on him? As much as she wanted to despise him, she couldn't. There was too much love in her heart for him, although she'd never look at him the same. In time, her love would die.

"We're not going to prison. We're innocent." Quinn patted her back.

"Do you truly think we'll get out of here?"

He nodded against her head. "Yes. I'll contact Mother tomorrow and have her get a good lawyer. They have no evidence against us."

Anna shuddered and cleared her throat. "Yes, they do."

eighteen

"Sheriff, open this door. I have the right to contact an attorney." Quinn shook the bars of his cell, his anger evident.

Anna hated the bars keeping them apart now. Her brother hadn't liked it when the sheriff had separated them last night, but at least Quinn, too, had a cot to sleep on, such as it was.

The key jingled on the other side of the wooden door. Balancing a tray of aromatic food, the sheriff stepped into the vault-like room that held the two cells. "Got you some lunch."

He slid a plate under the three-inch gap between the bottom of each cell door and the floor. Anna didn't know if she could eat. One night in the cell had been bad enough, but now the morning was gone and the long, dreary afternoon loomed ahead. There was nothing to do but watch Quinn pace and to stew over Brett's complete betrayal.

"I've contacted the U.S. marshal's office in Bismarck and hope to hear from him soon. Maybe he can clear up this mess," Sheriff Jones said.

Quinn rattled the bars then leaned his forehead against them. "I'm telling you, Sheriff, this is all a big mistake."

"That's what I told Marshal Wickham, but then he showed me that sketch."

"What sketch? And how do you even know that man is really a marshal? Did he have a badge?"

The sheriff disappeared into the outer room for a minute then came back carrying a paper. Anna knew it was the drawing of her, and her mouth went dry.

Sheriff Jones passed it through the bars to Quinn. He

unfolded it and stared; then he pivoted toward her. "It looks just like you." He crossed to the bars separating them and stared at her pendant. "It's the exact same necklace as the one you're wearing. How could a mistake like this happen?"

Anna shrugged. "I believe it is the fault of a particular bank clerk. He saw me sitting on the boardwalk after I'd collided with that robber. Gold coins had spilled onto my skirt and all around me. He tried to have me arrested, but another man told him I wasn't involved. He must have given my description to the authorities. Mother was there, but I don't know if a judge would believe her story since she's related to us."

Quinn forked his hand through his hair. "Going by this, I can see why Brett confused you for an outlaw, but that still doesn't justify what he did. After I went and gave him a job and all."

"Well, we'll get this straightened out soon." The sheriff reached for the picture and pocketed it. "I'm sorry to have to keep you folks here."

Anna jumped as the heavy wooden door thudded shut. In the dim lighting, she decided to rescue her lunch before the mice could get it. Quinn did the same, and his cot groaned as he sat.

"What did he bring us?" He tugged away the cloth covering the plate. "Mmm. . .pot roast."

Anna watched her brother wolf down the meat and vegetables. She speared a chunk of potato with her fork and nibbled one end. Food just didn't interest her.

"You won't have any of Leyna's cinnamon bread to snack on later, so eat up, sis."

"Do you think she knows? I wonder what the hands did when they couldn't find you."

Quinn lowered his plate to his lap and sighed. "I don't know. I hope they aren't out scouring the countryside, thinking I've been hurt."

"Maybe the sheriff could let the people at the ranch know what's going on."

"Good idea. I'll ask him when he comes back."

Anna poked at a carrot. "What I don't understand is how Brett could believe us guilty of killing his brother and robbing a bank. Hasn't he gotten to know us? Can't he see that we're good people?" Frustrated, she flung the tear off her cheek.

"It's a lawman's job to be objective."

"I can't believe you're defending him, big brother."

"I don't know how he even associated us with the Sallingers in the first place."

Anna heard a rustling and noticed two mice in the neighboring cell. A shiver charged down her spine. She tossed a bread crust through the metal slats that resembled wooden lattice.

"Hey! Don't encourage them."

She quirked a sad grin. "I'm just hoping to keep them over there."

"That's fine. They don't bother me." Quinn stomped his foot and the mice dashed under his cot. "Eat. You don't know when we'll get another meal, and it might not be as good as this one."

Anna managed to swallow about a third of her meal; then she offered the rest to her brother. He stabbed her meat through the bars and made quick order of finishing it before sliding his plate back under the cell door. Anna lay back on her cot, and Quinn resumed his pacing.

The jangling of the cell door jarred Anna awake. She yawned and sat up, smoothing her mussed hair with her hand.

"I don't know how to tell you how sorry I am for the mix-up. Got a telegram from Marshal Cronan in Bismarck. Turns out the real Sallinger gang is in custody down in Deadwood. They tried to rob a stage that held a payroll shipment, but it was actually filled with deputies. They caught the gang red-handed, and you're free to go with my deepest apologies."

Thank you, Lord! "Hurry, please, I need to get out of this horrid place."

The sheriff looked as if he'd eaten a bushel of green apples as he stepped back and let her pass. Then he unlocked Quinn's cell. "Miss McFarland, your wagon and Quinn's horse are at the livery. Marshal Wickham saw to them for you."

"Right nice of him." Quinn's sarcastic tone almost made Anna smile. "Ready to go home?" His brown eyes mirrored the relief she felt.

"All I can think of at the moment is a hot bath." Anna stepped into the sheriff's office and stared at her filthy hands. Her dress was a mass of wrinkles and as dirty as her palms. She dreaded going outside looking like this.

"I can get the wagon if you want to wait here." Quinn must have sensed her discomfort.

As ready as she was to be free of this place, when she looked out the window and saw people walking by, she nodded. "That's very considerate. Thank you."

Locked up in the cell, she'd had nothing to do but think of Brett. Here in the light of day, his betrayal seemed even bigger, more painful. How did a woman get over such an event?

The thing that hurt the most was that he could think her capable of such a deed. She was certain she'd seen affection, maybe even love in his gaze. But now she must forget about him.

The problem was. . .she had no idea how to go about doing that.

&

Brett stabled Jasper in the barn at the boardinghouse he normally stayed at while in Bismarck and then headed to the marshal's office. Needing time to think and allow his heart to adjust after seeing Lottie in that cell, he'd ridden Jasper to Dickinson and caught the train there. He'd chosen to return and ask Marshal Cronan to send some other deputies to bring Jack and Lottie to Bismarck, where they would stand trial. He simply didn't have it within him to do it.

The scrawny deputy who normally sat at the front desk was not there today. Brett heard the rustle of papers and the screech of Marshal Cronan's chair and knocked on the doorjamb. The marshal's gaze darted up, and his mustache twitched.

"Good to see you, Brett. Have a seat."

Brett obeyed, thinking how things had changed since the last time he'd sat in this chair. He'd been on the verge of an exciting change when he'd turned in his badge the day Taylor died. And he hadn't yet met the woman who now haunted his dreams.

"How you doin'?"

That was a loaded question. Brett shrugged. "All right, I guess. All things considered."

The marshal shook his head. "That was a mess in Medora, huh?"

Brett eyed the marshal. Did the man know he'd fallen in love with an outlaw? How could he, when Brett barely comprehended it himself?"

"Feels good to know the Sallingers are locked up, doesn't it?"

Brett nodded, still seeing Lottie's splotchy face with trails running across her cheeks where she'd wiped her face with hands dirtied from the jail cell. He hated thinking of her locked up where the sun couldn't glisten on her golden hair.

"What are you going to do now? Stay on the job or go back to your ranch?" The marshal locked his hands behind his head and leaned back, causing the chair to moan and groan under his bulk.

"I'm going home. It won't be the same without Taylor there, but I'm ready to settle down." His gaze traveled over the wanted posters stuck to the bulletin board out of habit, but he no longer had the heart to chase outlaws. In fact, the only way he knew he had a heart at all was that his was breaking. But in spite of the fact that he'd fallen in love with the outlaw he'd been trailing, he'd done his job and had seen the Sallingers captured. He just couldn't stand to sit back and watch Lottie be convicted.

"I don't suppose you'd consider waiting to retire long enough to go down with the team I'm sending to Deadwood to bring back the Sallingers? I figure you've earned the chance, even if you did chase a dead end."

"What?" Brett leaned forward in his chair, his mind swirling. "I left the Sallingers locked up in the Medora jail. How could they have gotten all the way to Deadwood in such a short time?"

Marshal Cronan leaned on his desk. "Where have you been, boy? I telegraphed the sheriff in Medora and told him to release that couple you'd arrested. We already had the Sallingers in Deadwood, caught red-handed trying to rob a decoy stage filled with marshals."

Brett's mouth hung open, his whole body numb. "But Anna McFarland was a dead ringer for that picture of Lottie. I tracked her right here from Bismarck, and she even wore the exact same necklace that Lottie wore in the sketch you gave me."

"Oh, that." The marshal sighed. "Seems the clerk who gave us that description was mistaken. He confused the woman Lottie ran into outside the bank with Lottie and gave us her description. I don't have to tell you that he's been fired. In fact, I talked with the banker this morning." The marshal twisted one end of his thick mustache. "Two days ago, an Ellen McFarland met with the bank president and gave him a draft for forty cash dollars to replace two double eagles that had fallen accidentally into her daughter's handbag after she and that outlaw collided outside the bank."

Brett leaned back in his chair, taking it all in. Unbelievable joy battled with pure regret. His Anna wasn't a thief. Only she wasn't his Anna and never would be after what he'd done.

"You look like you've seen a ghost. What's wrong? I thought you'd be happy."

"I put two innocent people in jail. Why would I be happy about that?"

"If that gal is the spitting image of the drawing, how could you have known?"

Brett stood and reached into his pocket, pulling out the two double eagle coins. "And she had these in her possession." He dropped them on the desk. One spun around before hitting the other coin and falling down.

The marshal ran his thumb over the notched edge. "These are the double eagles she mentioned in her letter. How did you get them?"

"I confiscated them when she tried to spend them in a Medora store." Brett huffed a laugh. "It's ironic, isn't it? I jailed Anna McFarland for stealing these coins, and then I took them from her when they legally belonged to her. I've sure made a mess of things."

The marshal stood and looked him in the eye. "I can see why you did what you did. You had two solid forms of evidence. Those folks are free now, so don't worry about it. I'll see that they get this money back."

Brett knew he would worry. He'd sacrificed his future for a mistake. "I'd turn in my badge, but I lost it in that bear attack I wrote you about."

The marshal waved his hand in the air, stirring up the lingering smoke from his last cigar. He stepped around the side of his desk and held out his hand. "Don't worry about the badge. I've got plenty more. Looks like you've recovered all right from your injuries."

Rubbing a hand across his chest, Brett nodded. His chest had healed, but his heart was another subject.

"I wish you luck, Wickham."

Brett shook the marshal's hand and headed toward the boardinghouse. After a soak in a hot tub, he sat on the end of his bed, staring out the window. How had he made such a mess of things? If only he'd never gone in that Bismarck store and seen Lott—no, Anna—none of this would have ever happened.

But then he'd never have gotten to know her or fallen in love. Brett fell to his knees. "Oh, God, how could I have let my quest for vengeance go so far? I knew in my heart that Anna wasn't capable of the things I accused her of. Forgive me for charging ahead and taking things into my own hands. Please, God, let Anna forgive me."

For the next hour, he prayed and cried out to God. Never again did he want to walk in his own power without God's guidance. But the thing God was now requiring of him was more than difficult, although he knew it had to be done.

He stood and walked to the window, knowing he'd be on the next train to Medora. He owed Quinn and Anna a huge apology. He had to make things right with them—and he hoped he didn't get shot in the process.

nineteen

Anna sat beside the creek with her rifle across her lap. She seriously doubted the bear would be back after Sam told her how he and Hank had found her and the cub and had chased them several miles away, but she wasn't taking any chances.

After spending twenty-four hours locked in a tiny jail cell, she couldn't get enough of God's creation. The night she and Quinn returned home after their release, she'd sat on the porch watching the sunset. Even later, she'd gone outside to stare at the stars.

Now she watched the water gently lapping over the stones in the creek bed. Its soft sounds ministered to her aching soul. How could she miss Brett so much after what he'd done?

But hadn't he just been doing his job? Even if his train was on the wrong track?

She exhaled deeply. Hours of prayer, begging God to take away her love for him, had been a futile effort so far. Maybe it just took more time.

She longed to see him again but wasn't sure what she'd do if she did. Quinn was still mad, though seeing that sketch of her had soothed him some. A grin tugged at her mouth. It was her opinion that her tough brother was more angered over the fact that Brett had bested him and then sneaked him off the ranch with nobody the wiser. Few men were tougher than Quinn and big enough to outfight him.

Two gray rock doves drifted down to the edge of the creek and strutted around, their necks a shiny iridescent green and purple in the afternoon sunlight. They pecked at the ground for a few minutes as Anna watched. A magpie swooped down and landed off to her right. It squawked at her as if telling her this was his domain. He ducked his head and pecked at something shiny. Anna stood, wondering what would be reflecting the sun in such a way. The bird chattered but flew off a few yards when she walked in its direction. Anna knew what she'd found the moment her fingers touched the slick metal. Brett's badge.

She wrapped her hand around it and didn't try to stop the tears. How could she still love him when he'd thought so little of her?

After a few minutes, she stuck the badge in her pocket. She would hide it away, knowing it would always be a memento of the man she'd loved. As she rode up to the ranch a short while later, she saw Quinn standing in front of the barn with Hank and Claude beside him. Quinn and Hank aimed their rifles toward the side of the barn, while Claude looked to be trying to calm her brother. What was going on? Had a coyote come looking for their chickens?

"Get off my land."

She reined Bella to a stop and slid off. As she hurried to her brother's side, a rider came into view. Anna gasped. Brett.

"I told you to leave. You've got a lot of nerve showing up here after what you did." Quinn lifted his rifle, showing he meant business.

Her rebellious heart leaped in recognition. Now all she had to do was decide if she wanted to shoot him or hug him.

Out of the corner of her eye, Anna saw Leyna come out onto the porch, holding her broom as if she wanted in on the action. Anna pulled her gaze back to Brett, and her heart somersaulted. He was so handsome. His blue eyes, so vivid against his tanned skin, couldn't seem to stray from her face. His expression begged for compassion. His longish hair hung down against his collar. His Stetson was pushed back on his forehead, revealing the lighter skin along his dark hairline.

Oh, how she loved this man, but could she ever trust him again?

❧

Brett's outlaw heart lurched as Anna rode up. He needed to keep his wits about him, but his gaze kept straying to her. She looked so much better than the last time he'd seen her, and for that, he was thankful. It had nearly gutted him seeing her suffering so much. He held up his hand to Quinn. "Please hear me out. I've come to apologize."

"We don't want your apology. We opened our home to you and tended your wounds when you were half dead. Then you tossed my sister and me in jail."

Anna lifted her hand to her brother's arm. "Quinn, put the rifle down. You know you're not going to shoot a U.S. marshal."

Quinn darted a glare her direction. "Stay out of this, Anna."

Brett reached for his shirt pocket. "Just let me show you the sketch that started all this."

Quinn lowered his rifle but didn't relax his rigid stance. "I saw it. But after you got to know us, you should have known we couldn't do something like rob a bank, much less kill someone."

Brett pocketed the drawing with a sigh and leaned forward, arms resting across his saddle horn. "I'll admit I struggled with it all. I was ready to ride away, thinking there'd been some mistake—had even wired my superior that this was a dead end—when Anna plopped down those stolen coins at the mercantile. It was evidence I couldn't ignore."

Quinn sighed. "You could have talked to us about it."

Brett took a risk and dismounted. "A lawman doesn't discuss his case with the criminal he's investigating."

Quinn raised his rifle again. "We aren't criminals."

Brett lifted his palms in a sign of surrender. "I know that now, and for what it's worth, I'm deeply sorry about my error and the trouble it caused. You have no idea how sorry."

"You've said your piece; now get goin'." Quinn hiked his chin and glared at Brett.

Anna's brother would never forgive him. "I've repented to God, but I want you to know that if I sought vengeance for my brother's death instead of justice, I'm sorry for that, too."

Quinn relaxed his stance. "I'm sorry about your brother. It must be tough to lose one."

Brett nodded. "Taylor was only nineteen. He had his whole life ahead of him."

Quinn looked Brett in the eye. Caring for younger siblings was something Anna's brother could relate to.

"Well. . .thank you for letting me apologize. I want you to know I'm deeply sorry."

"We get the idea." Quinn looked at Hank, who stood just inside the barn, and swiped his arm in the air. The cowhand lowered his rifle, and he and Claude went into the barn.

Unable to read Anna's expression, Brett hoped and prayed she'd be willing to talk to him. He looked back at Quinn. "I'd like to have a private word with Anna, if you don't mind."

A muscle ticked in Quinn's jaw as he looked at his sister. Anna gazed at Brett with apprehension but nodded.

Quinn glared at Brett. "Don't break her heart again, or so help me, lawman or not, I'll come gunnin' for you."

❧

Anna couldn't stop wringing her hands as she and Brett stopped by the pasture fence. She never dreamed she'd be walking with him ever again, much less so soon after what had happened.

"Anna. . ."

She loved her name on his lips. "You know, you never called me by my first name when you were here before."

Brett ducked his head. "I wanted to, but I had to keep

thinking of you as Lottie, in order to keep my distance."

Hope flickered in her chest like a match to kindling. "Why did you need to keep your distance?"

Brett looked her in the eye, and a sad smile bent the edges of his mouth. "I think you know. It was all I could do not to fall head over heels in love with you."

Just that fast her hopes sank. So he didn't love her. She closed her eyes and willed her tears away. She could get through this without breaking down, and she'd forgive him so he could get on with his life. Without her.

"I'm so sorry for all the trouble I caused. If you only knew how I'd struggled, arguing with myself that you couldn't possibly be Lottie. It wasn't until I saw those coins that I actually believed it. In fact, I was ready to ride out that very day and go back to Bismarck."

"Well. . .it's over now, so stop apologizing. Are you going to keep marshaling?"

He leaned his arm across the top of a fence post and stared at the horses grazing in the field. "I retired. I'm going home."

Anna tried to not show her disappointment. Had she read him totally wrong? Hadn't she seen love in his gaze, or had she just imagined it?

"Well. . .I guess that's it then. I wish you good luck, and maybe if you ever get in this area you could stop by." She stiffened her spine and held out her hand.

Brett looked at it then at her face, his gaze questioning. He stood and took her hand, then wrapped his other hand over the top of hers. "Anna. . .I can't leave without telling you how I feel."

Her heart skipped a beat.

"I know I have no right to say this, but I'll always regret it if I don't. I love you." His warm blue eyes told her his words were true.

Anna gasped, and the tears she'd held at bay broke loose.

"Oh, Brett, I thought I'd lost you." She fell into his arms, and he held her tight.

"I know, darlin'. I felt the same way." He rested his head on hers and watched a half-grown foal frolicking in the tall grass. This was what he wanted, her by his side for the rest of his life.

She leaned back. "You have to know I love you, too." Anna stroked his cheek, and he leaned into her touch.

"I don't deserve your love, especially after what I did."

She pressed her fingers against his lips, surprised at their softness. "Shh. . .don't say that. Love is a gift from God."

Brett recaptured her hand. "Isn't it amazing how God can take such a mess and work something good from it? If I hadn't had that poster and then seen you in the store in Bismarck, we never would have met."

Anna nodded. "That's true, isn't it? God is truly amazing."

"You're amazing. I can't believe you'd forgive me so easily." He ran his hand down her soft cheek. "Anna, do you have it in your heart to marry a scoundrel like me?"

She couldn't stop her chin from quivering. Brett's loving gaze turned worried. She had to put the man out of his misery. "Yes, I'll marry you, Deputy Marshal Wickham."

He grinned, leaning in closer. "It's Mr. Wickham, ma'am. I turned in my resignation."

His lips touched hers, and their kiss was all she had dreamed it could be. He held her tight against his solid chest, and she felt cherished and protected. To think she'd almost lost him. He deepened his kiss with a promise of many more to come.

Suddenly, a shot rang out, hitting the fence post three feet away, sending splinters of wood flying. Anna and Brett leaped apart.

"Hey, that's my sister you're sparking with, Mister." Quinn raised his rifle as if preparing to fire again.

Brett leaned his head against hers. "Your family sure keeps things interesting."

She returned his grin. "Yes, Mr. Wickham, they do at that."

epilogue

Anna fidgeted with her autumn flower bouquet. Quinn paced the back of the church, waiting to escort her down the aisle. He'd asked her half a dozen times if she was sure that she wanted to marry the man who'd tossed her in jail. But she was certain. Not a doubt lingered in her mind.

Brett had offered to stay until spring to help on the Rocking M to make sure he'd smoothed things over with Quinn. In April, providing there wasn't deep snow, she and her husband would travel to his Bar W Ranch in southwestern North Dakota. While she was happy to spend time with her family, she was eager to have Brett all to herself. Being a newlywed and living in the same home as her watchful brother would present some challenges. She could only hope that Quinn would honor her and Brett's vows and not pester him once they were married.

She peeked around the corner and saw Adam and Mariah sitting in the front row, along with her mother and grandmother. Mariah looked over her shoulder, caught Anna's eye, and waved. Anna smiled back. Just last night at dinner, Adam had broken the news that Mariah was with child. They, too, would be wintering at the ranch, and everyone would enjoy the new baby, come March. Anna couldn't help wondering how long it would be before she and Brett had a child of their own.

Only a handful of their friends had made the trip to Bismarck for the wedding, but Anna didn't mind. She rather liked the coziness of the small group in the chapel of her grandmother's church.

The organist started playing, and she heard a door open and close. Quinn looked around the corner of the chapel's entryway and then nodded at her. "It's not too late to change your mind, sis."

She smacked him on the sleeve. "I want to marry Brett. When will you get it through that fat head of yours?"

He grinned, looking so much like her father that a lump formed in her throat.

"Quinn, I know it hasn't been easy on you since Pa died, but I want you to know that I'm deeply grateful for all your hard work to make the ranch a success and how you helped Mama to keep Adam and me on the straight and narrow. I hope one day that God will bring a beautiful woman into your life and that you'll find the happiness I have."

"Goodness, sis, you're gonna make me cry." He looped her arm around his. "Let's go make that scoundrel down there happy. He looks as nervous as a mustang fresh off the range."

She smiled, and as she rounded the corner, her gaze captured her beloved's. Brett looked so handsome in the dark suit that matched his hair. She hoped all her children had his hair and beautiful blue eyes—all but one ornery tomboy who loved split skirts and riding full-gallop.

Brett's wide smile warmed her heart. She breathed a thankful prayer to God for forgiveness. Without it, today would never have happened.

Quinn acted as if he didn't want to hand her over, but she knew her brother was just playing. "Make sure you get the ceremony right, preacher, or this fellow might toss you in jail."

The minister cast a bewildered glance from Quinn to Brett. The audience chuckled as Quinn sat down next to his mother. Brett took Anna's hand and turned her to face the preacher. Joy overflowed as she said her vows to love and cherish forever the man God had given her.

ॐ

April 1895

"All aboard!" The conductor waved at the final passengers who still lingered on the platform.

"You ready, Mrs. Wickham?"

Anna nodded, afraid if she voiced the words that she'd break into tears, and she didn't want her husband thinking that she loved her family more than him. But leaving her family, the Rocking M, Medora, and everything familiar to journey to the unknown was scary. At least Leyna was coming with her. Brett had said he'd starve to death if he had to rely on Anna's cooking, but she knew that he didn't want her to be too lonely. Leyna's cousin would be coming to cook for Quinn after Adam and Mariah left again next month.

Her family gathered around, and she hugged each one. Her mother had come to visit the baby and to see her off. She clutched her twin, hating to turn him loose now that she'd had him back for a time, but he no longer belonged to her. She released Adam, kissed baby Jonathon, and hugged Mariah.

With tears in her eyes, her mother handed her a package wrapped in brown paper.

"What's this?" Anna reached for it and clasped her mother's hand.

"Mariah and I finished the quilt. You'd done so much work on it this winter that we wanted it finished so you could take it to your new home."

"Oh, thank you both." She fell into her mother's arms, wondering when she'd see her again. The train whistle wailed, and they stepped apart. "You will come and visit?"

Her mother nodded and wiped her tears. Brett helped Leyna onto the train and handed up her satchel. He came to

Anna's side, holding his hand lightly against her back. Anna gazed at Quinn. They'd become much closer since being locked in jail together, and now she hated to leave him. If only he had a wife and family. That item still topped her prayer list, and she knew God would be faithful.

"Good-bye, Quinn." Her chin quivered.

"Don't you dare cry, sis, or you just might see a grown man weep." He embraced her in a fierce bear hug then abruptly turned her loose. He looked at Brett and held out his hand. "You'd better take good care of her. I still have a loaded shotgun handy."

Brett smiled. "I'd give my life for hers and have the scars to prove it."

Quinn grinned and hugged Brett, both men slapping each other on the shoulder.

"Final call! All aboard."

"Good-bye, everyone. You'd better write." Anna allowed Brett to help her up the steps to the railcar, then hurried to her seat and plastered her face against the window. How was it possible to be so excited to be going to a new home when it was so hard to leave the old one? Brett settled in beside her and draped his arm over her shoulders.

"We'll be back, princess, and they'll come to visit." He kissed her temple, sending tingles down her neck and arm. How could he still affect her so much after six months of marriage?

She smiled at him. "I know. Don't fret. I want to be with *you*, remember?"

His gaze said he wished they were alone instead of on a crowded train. He dipped down and kissed her lightly on the lips.

Leyna tsk-tsked at them. She sat in the seat facing theirs, wielding her wooden spoon and an ornery grin.

A sputtery laugh slipped from Anna's lips. Brett chuckled and shook his head. Anna looked out and waved a final good-bye to her family as the train left the station.

The train shuddered as it picked up speed. They were on their way to a new future, and Anna couldn't wait to explore it.

A Letter To Our Readers

Dear Reader:
In order that we might better contribute to your reading
enjoyment, we would appreciate your taking a few minutes
to respond to the following questions. We welcome your
comments and read each form and letter we receive. When
completed, please return to the following:

Fiction Editor
Heartsong Presents
PO Box 719
Uhrichsville, Ohio 44683

1. Did you enjoy reading *Outlaw Heart* by Vickie McDonough?
   ❏ Very much! I would like to see more books by this author!
   ❏ Moderately. I would have enjoyed it more if

   _____

   _____

   _____

2. Are you a member of **Heartsong Presents**? ❏ Yes ❏ No
   If no, where did you purchase this book? _____

   _____

3. How would you rate, on a scale from 1 (poor) to 5 (superior),
   the cover design? _____

4. On a scale from 1 (poor) to 10 (superior), please rate the
   following elements.

   ____ Heroine   ____ Plot
   ____ Hero   ____ Inspirational theme
   ____ Setting   ____ Secondary characters

5. These characters were special because? _____
_____
_____

6. How has this book inspired your life? _____
_____
_____

7. What settings would you like to see covered in future
   Heartsong Presents books? _____
_____
_____

8. What are some inspirational themes you would like to see
   treated in future books? _____
_____
_____

9. Would you be interested in reading other **Heartsong
   Presents** titles? ❑ Yes ❑ No

10. Please check your age range:
        ❑ Under 18   ❑ 18-24
        ❑ 25-34   ❑ 35-45
        ❑ 46-55   ❑ Over 55

Name _____
Occupation _____
Address _____
City, State, Zip_____

MISSOURI
Brides

3 stories in 1

Hope is renewed in three historical romances by Mildred Colvin. Missouri of the early 1800s is full of exciting growth, but for three women, it is filled with lost hopes.

Historical, paperback, 368 pages, 5³/₁₆" x 8"

Presents

Great Inspirational Romance at a Great Price!

Heartsong Presents books are inspirational romances in contemporary and historical settings, designed to give you an enjoyable, spirit-lifting reading experience. You can choose wonderfully written titles from some of today's best authors like Wanda E. Brunstetter, Mary Connealy, Susan Page Davis, Cathy Marie Hake, Joyce Livingston, and many others.

When ordering quantities less than twelve, above titles are $2.97 each.
Not all titles may be available at time of order.